Don't put it all the way in.

Surviving
a
Female Stalker

Don't put it all the way in.

Surviving
a
Female Stalker

Seven M.

Surviving a Female Stalker.

Published by Revamp Media Group,
P.O. Box 477
Raritan, New Jersey 08869

Author: Muhammad, Seven
Paper back: ISBN 978-0-9890739-0-5
EBook: ISBN 978-0-9890739-1-2
•   Surviving A Female Stalker

Published 2013
Edited by Seven Muhammad
Cover Photo by Melanie T. Coney
Production Coordinated by Revamp Media Group

Visit Seven Muhammad www.mrseven.com for more insightful information.

Dedication

This one is for the woman who never learned to focus and got put out in four feet of snow with one boot on. To the ones who mistreat their own children because a man won't be friends with them. To the one who is facing a lawsuit and criminal charges for filing a false felony police report. To Tampa who lied about everything she could until she got caught, including the fact that she lived with a man while trying to marry me. You were one of the worst ever.

To all the bat-shit crazy women who make sane women look bad, thanks for the lessons.

And to the sane and very beautiful woman who loves and supports my work-1 love you deeply. You will be my wife soon.

You have my word.

Foreword

BY DUANE HARRIS

My name is Duane Harris, fifty one years old. Currently living in Mahwah, New Jersey by way of Harlem and I am a Black man. When a good friend of mine asked me to do the foreword for his book, I found it interesting. First, because I was asked and second on the topic that I was talking to him about one night in a club about a girl. Who, for the lack of a better phrase, was smitten. I saw that the girl made him uncomfortable because she was pretty much over the top, all the way in, head over heels-whatever you want to say but I noticed that it made him uncomfortable. My friend Seven M kind of made it seem like he was mad at her. So I looked at the situation and I said to myself, now why would you be mad at her? It's not her fault that she's lost her mind over you. If you're going to blame someone, you've got to start with you. He looked at me like he was wondering what I was talking about. I had to explain to him. Now, how you gonna be mad at her when you put the whole thing in? I know that's what happened. You shoulda put in half. Once you put the whole thing in there's nothing left. I found that when you're dealing with a woman and she starts going nuts and doing all those things, at some point, you must take responsibility for what you created. The woman is only going to be the partner you create. And yea, I know it sounds crude for me to say-don't put it all the way in, but that's pretty much all it comes down to.

I would like to thank my friend Seven M for letting me put the foreword on his book.

Table of Contents

SURVIVING A FEMALE STALKER

Preface

First of all, I know that some of our women are upset because they don't like the title of this work. Don't judge this book by what you read on the cover. This is not and was never meant to be some latent misogynistic women-bashing book. We don't do that around here. The fact is, most men don't have their shit together either.

SURVIVING A FEMALE STALKER

Introduction

Stalk'er n 2. one who moves in a menacing or threatening fashion.

Stalk (stok) v 1. to pursue by tracking

Time to explore some bad behavior on the part of human beings based on some shit that most of us can't control- our feelings. T o look at some of the irrational shit that transpires between people when the misunderstanding about why we are together-becomes a beef. This has been a hard code for most to decipher because the bad behavior and the good behavior come from the same wish list. The very same behavior that makes you feel secure, loved, protected and free will have you scared, hurt, ass-out and locked up somewhere. The only variable is the other person involved.

Example:

Here is a good story. You meet someone, fall in love and live your life as partners. You are sexually compatible and you can talk to them about anything. You do everything together, go everywhere together and make all decisions based on how it will affect the other person's life. He or she surprises you for lunch, sends small gifts, balloons and flowers to your job. Leaves you instant messages and forwards e-mails about love and relationships. They make sure they never let more than a couple hours go by without a call or a message about how much they love you. Every voice-mail and text is about how they would do anything to spend the rest of their lives with you. How no one will ever come between you. They attend all your events, support all your dreams and show up at your job. They wake up in the middle of the night, call you to tell you about the dream they just had. They are with you and the feeling of being left by yourself is gone because there is someone who thinks of you and nothing else. The only thing in the world that they are focused on is you. This is the good stuff. The stuff movies and love songs are made of.

Okay, we got that out of the way.

Now here's the bad story. You meet someone that you like and you decide to become sex partners. You are physically compatible and they are cool to talk to. You discuss the fact that there are no future plans and you both agree that this is what you both want. You are never seen in public together, you don't hang out and you never consult with this person when it comes to future plans. Then one of you decides for whatever reason that the relationship has run its course and the other one will not accept it. This crazy motherfucker won't back off. They don't have any intention of honoring the grownup agreement and now they won't go away! They pop up at your work during lunch hours, they keep sending unwanted gifts to your job. Sending balloons and flowers with creepy notes and forwarding all these dumb-ass stories of love beyond all odds to your e-mail. They won't let two hours go by without leaving a voice-mail or sending you some crazy-ass text message. Every message is the same. How they will never leave you alone, how no one will ever come between you. How they will never stop showing up at your events, and how they won't stop involving themselves in your future business endeavors. They call you all times of the night and break your sleep at will, and all hopes of you being left alone are shot because this crazy fucker won't focus on shit else but you. This is the bad shit. The shit court dates and police reports are made of.

See what I mean? The behavior and attention shown are the same but the difference is: in the good story, the attention was welcomed. In the bad story, the attention was un-welcomed. Same behavior, same intent, wrong person. Unfortunately you have made yourself victim and you are the one who has to take responsibility for placing yourself in this position.

In this work you will find not only my own story of survival, but interviews with other men who have similar experience. I decided to do it this way so there would be nothing lopsided, to supply the reader with more than one point of view. According to national law enforcement averages as of 2009, the case of violent female stalkers has gone up 38% in 16 years. That's a big jump. In fact, Lifetime network aired a whole day of female stalker movies to "commemorate" that fact just last summer. Of course we have always been aware that stalking wasn't exclusive to males but the numbers regarding women who stalk have been ignored until Eileen Warnos. Movies like "The Burning Bed" and the home removal of a working penis by Mrs. Elena Bobbit, only addressed some heroic violent strike against some male abuser or chronic womanizer. What about the violence and crazy shit being leveled against good dudes? Stand up men? Honest dudes?

After all the research and interviews, we have come up with three basic rules to help safeguard you from being a victim of a stalker, in this case, a female stalker.

SEVEN M.

Three Basic Rules

1. Never have sex of any kind with a woman who is attracted to you if you don't feel the same about her. That's some careless, dumb- ass, selfish shit to do. So, if there is absolutely no chance that you will ever want to have a real relationship with her, keep your dick to yourself.

2. Never ever show up to a major holiday or family gathering with a woman that wants to be with you if the feelings aren't mutual. Thanksgiving, Christmas parties at the family home or playing escort for her 30 birthday party are an absolute fucking no no!!!

3. Never mix money with a woman you're not going to stay with and never mix money with a woman that you're not married to. Shit, the bottom line is, never mix money.

SURVIVING A FEMALE STALKER

Chapter 1

Interview 1 Subject A

Q. Subject A, what is your age, nationality and birthplace?

A. 46 yrs old, Cuban, Dominican, Italian birthplace Fordham Hospital, Bronx New York.

Q. How did you meet her?

A. In a club.

Q. How long were you dealing with her?

A. About four months.

Q. How old was she when you met and how old were you?

A. I wanna say I was 27 and she was about 24.

Q. Did she have any children?

A. No, no children.

Q. So she's 24, no children right?

A. Right.

Q. What was her nationality?

A. Black and Dominican.

Q. Did you live together at any point during those four months?

A. No.

Q. How was your sex life?

A. Sex was excellent. Over the top.

Q. Over the top? Okay, beautiful. That is usually the first problem. Was there any violent or aggressive behavior, either on your part or her part during those four months?

A. Well just to be brief, in the beginning when I was throwing her the dick, it seemed as if everything was going well, and then she wanted more, more, and more. At that time I had other chicks that I was dealing with, so I wasn't basically a one man chick at that time. You know she wanted more of my time, which started to become a problem, the start of the problem.

Q. Sex over the top right? What made you say that?

A. Cause she licked.... (STARTS LAUGHING)

Q. Oh okay got you, you want to stop right there?

A. I'll share the story...

Q. Let's go.

A. First chick like chick to really go in on me...start off licking the ass, I was like wow. So she caught me out there for a min, and then once I thrashed her, then I reversed the role. I had her, but she caught me off guard because, I don't uh, a lot of men ain't really into that. It happened quickly the first time I was like wow, but uh yeah and she did everything, the toes, ass, she went in, she went in. She was a freak...just like one the females that was very open.

2

SEVEN M.

Q. Remember when I asked did ya'll live together when all this thrashing and other goings on was happening.... where were ya'll?

A. Hotel

Q. Hotel, okay. I gotta ask you man. At any time did you think or feel like either of you were feeling anything more than just the physical?

A. Nah I never felt it. I just loved fucking her, to be honest, the pussy was excellent I just you know, I admit she had me caught but I wouldn't allow her to really, because I had other women like I said when I felt I was getting to caught up with her, I just fall back. And she don't understand that, cause I don't know whether she was dealing with someone else, while she was dealing with me, but you know, that part never came up. So, she was the one who started to be like where you at, this that and the third, why you not spending time with me, ahhyayayaya...

Q. So, ya'll meet at different spots?

A. Umm hum

Q. Sex life is great, you saying she's Dominican and Black, and I happen to know you personally so I know what your taste is, and I am sure that everything was as it should be. So now I have to ask you again, it's the same question, but I'm gonna ask it another way...Did you feel like at any point like she was starting to fall in love?

A. Yeah, cause she stabbed me.

Q. Okay, so you have to tell me about that one, cause that's the next question. Was there any violent behavior?

A. She caught me coming out of a movie theatre with another young lady, ran up on me and stabbed me in my shoulder. And was like you lying motherfucker... I am in shock; I see a knife sticking out of my shoulder I'm like bitch is you crazy? So I go to snatch the bitch up, and the young lady that I'm with is like no, let me handle this, and they went at it. And luckily the other chick I was with at the theatre had her skills up.

Q. So what movie theatre are we talking about?

A. It was on 89 and 3 Ave, what is that a Loews? It's been a minute since that whole incident.

Q. I know the one you're talking about. At any point did she say that she loved you? Did you tell her that ya'll where going to be together?

A. Yeah well, when I would fall back on the sex she would be like why you not spending time with me...I love you...I want to have your baby...I thought we were going to be a family....I'm like family? I had another chick. I was like come on Ma. Now you getting senile on a motherfucker, you know what I mean?

Q. So you had the discussion with her?

A. Absolutely. But she wanted me to be hers and that is what she wanted.

Q. And during the discussion did she agree to what you told her?

A. No, basically she was in denial. But honestly, the more I said it, the more she was like nah you're not seeing anybody. I was like yeah, yeah, I am, she was like, no, and you're not!

SEVEN M.

She was like I will hurt you, but I'm thinking come on, I ain't got you like that. You know what I am saying and I was like you 24 and she was a bad bitch. I mean my swag was up but I just couldn't really figure out how I could have her in the space that she was...

Q. Before the stabbing incident, did she show any signs of aggression?

A. She poured acid on my car,

Q. What do you mean?

A. She threw some shit on my car that peeled the paint off my shit Q. How long were you dealing with her?

A. Yo, I was with the chick for about four months. The first three months was beautiful, everything was beautiful. Soon as I started laying back off the dick I started seeing signs of it....and I would go out and see her out at events that I was at...movie screenings...clubs parties...she would be everywhere I went..I'm like does this bitch have a bug on me or some shit? I thought she was FBI or something at one point, cause I couldn't understand how she knew my every move...

Q. Wow, wait a min, you see her at three different places?

A. It was more like, well the theatre was one, Halo was another spot, what's that joint, Paladium?

Q. That's three.

A. It might have been a few more but, I don't remember the place and times so I don't want to sound like I am exaggerating,

Q. That is stalking...three places is enough.

A. Yeah and then she would show up at my mom's Q. Just show up?

A. My mom's had to come out and say, "Darling you. Better leave him alone." My mom had to step to her. "My mom had to come outside and say: "darling, what are doing out in front of my house?" She was like; I am waiting for your son. My mom's says, my son is not here and you have to leave. Then my mom would like call me and say, yeah she left son.

Q. That's terrible. Was that love?

A. I think she was more obsessed than in love. I don't know how at what point do you consider yourself a stalker? At what point? After the second time, third time, fourth time? Twice is too many times for me.

Q. She stabbed you?

A. She stabbed me in my arm

Q. At a movie theatre. So there is a bunch of people around?

A. Absolutely,

Q. Alright, so she stabbed you in public in front of a whole bunch of people not caring about the consequences, which means that she doesn't care what happens to her afterwards, she's just going to stab you because you are out with another chick.

A. I was coming out of a theatre hugging a chick and the next thing I know there is a fucking knife sticking out of my shoulder. If you want to see the scar I can show you.

Q. And there is another one when she poured acid on your car and peeled the paint?

A. Right

SEVEN M.

Q. That's aggressive behavior

A. Yeah I really don't know what material she used

Q. I know what material she used

A. But my front hood my back hood the shit leaked on it looked like crabs on my car...the paint was just like bubbling...! Was like what the fucK?

Q. What kind of car was it?

A. It was a, what kind of car did I have at that time....it was a Black 300Z...

Q. Was there any early indication that she would actually carry out her earlier threat to hurt you?

A. I realized that bitch was crazy when she stabbed me, so before then, no. She started out sane, like that move right there was like; oh I gotta get away from this bitch. I said, so how you gonna stab a nigga at the movie theatre in public? Right then and there I was like, oh shit...what the fuck is going on...so from that point on, I was ducking and...She caught a serious beat down and she continues...she did the car she came to my mom's house she you know, calling my phone a hundred times leaving crazy ass messages...

Q. Wait, what kind of messages?

A. How could you do this to me you mother fucker. I hate you...l hate you! Then me being a smart ass called her up and was like what's wrong with you? She was like; you know that the fuck is wrong with me. I was like, is the dick that good? She was like, don't play with me....don't play with me...you think it's a fucking game! I was like, if I got to go through this, I'm gonna have to send someone to see you. You already caught a beat down....ya know what I am saying....and I am pretty sure...ya know, I mean, you don't want to go any further...so please stop

I'm gonna tell you like this, I'm gonna go the legal route and go to the police

Q. NICE

A. And I'm gonna see how you gonna act and she was like, I don't give a fuck what you do. Man, when she did the stab thing, that told me that she didn't give a fuck so I had to throw the police out there but I never did call the police...l just put it out there...

Q. You usually don't have to....

A. So I got big sis on her...

Q. Whoa!

A. Yeah had to get big sis.

Q. I think you did the right thing.

A. After big sis had a couple of words with her...l ain't never heard from that bitch again...

Q. So that's how you got out?

A. That's how I got out....

Q. Big sis got you out.

A. Big sis got me out alright. I love my big sis (laughing).

Q. Mine too. Mine's about this tall, she's got a mean straight right....Knock a nigga straight out, but this is the thing though, this is the most important thing. What we're doing right now is really about helping people.

A. Oh wait I forgot an incident....

Q. Another incident? I need it I need it...

SEVEN M.

A. One time I was at one of the clubs...I got totally drunk....drunk out of my mind...Out my mind. I had my man drop me at my spot, he dropped me, he takes my car. I wake up this bitch on top of me fucking me....

Q. Oh shit, the same chick?

A. Yes!

Q. Wow

A. And peep this; my cousin was in my room on the floor...

Q. What the fuck?

A. One of my little cousin's mans was at my house chillin. This bitch broke in my apartment man she comes through the fire escape, she climbed up the fire escape got in my shit. I woke up, this bitch was fucking me, and this bitch was on top of me fucking me. My cousin was in there and said, "I woke up and saw a big light skinned ass going all up and down" (laughing)... I woke up I was like, hey what the fuck are you doing bitch?! She was like I'm gonna get me some...1 was like yo you are fucking out of your mind!

Q. So you what your really saying is you were sexually assaulted by this broad?

A. Yo, me and my cousin had to like grab this bitch up.

Q. You like Denzel in "Ricochet". Motherfucker wake up there's a broad bouncing up and down and he's like what the fuck?

A. Yeah man, I totally forgot that one...till this day I still don't know how she got into the apartment...the only way she could have gotten in there was through the fire escape, there is security on the door ya know what I mean.. Had me bugging. I was on the third floor...

Q. That's crazy man...so we got that and we know how you got out. Big sis got you out. What this is really about is, men being able to see themselves in these true stories to know what they should do different. I need the reversal, what would you do different?

A. Sometimes... and I'm gonna keep it straight-.sometimes there is no reversal. There's a getting out, but sometimes there's just no reversal. I mean it didn't matter I don't think it would have mattered how I went about this chick. I don't think it would have mattered because it was all lovely the first three months the fourth month like I said when I fell back with the dick because I felt/was getting caught up I was like, let me slow my roll and then she flipped. At that point, like I said, everything was good until I didn't want to hit it no more and that's when everything changed. On this situation, I don't think it would have gone any other way.

Q. Right

A. But I can at least give some insight if a chick acts out of order quickly then she will be out of order down the line.

Q. Yeah, you right.

A. You just have to use your mind and your heart and try to understand the person that you're dealing with. That's all. That's the best advice that I can give to the young men that are out there.

Q. So basically you're telling them to take a better look before they get involved.

A. Yeah. Just don't want to throw the dick because sometimes when you throw the dick, you may throw it too far.

Q. Exactly... (Laughing)

SEVEN M.

A. One more thing, my uncle always said don't always put it all the way in.(laughing)

7M. Alright. Thank you subject A!

Chapter 2

Interview 2 Subject B

Q. Subject B, state your name, age, nationality and birthplace.

A. I'm 45, African American and I was born in Norfolk Virginia and lived in VA beach most of my life.

Q. Thanks for coming through. You are here to share a story about an incident that you had with a woman. The questions start now.

Q. How did you meet her?

A. I was invited to a barbeque and I was going into the place and so was she. On the way in, I noticed the tents in the back, I saw this woman and went back to snatch my brother out the car, and that's how we met.

Q. How long were you involved?

A. We were involved for about two years.

Q. When you met, how old was she and how old were you?

A. She was 30 and I was 23 or 24 at the time.

Q. Did she have any children?

A. No, she didn't have any children.

Q. And what was her nationality?

A. She was Trinidadian and Jamaican.

Q. During this time, what were the living arrangements? Did she live with you or did you live with her?

A. She had her own place and I had mine. Then after the first year, we said ok, let's do it together, and she moved in with me. Q. And after she moved in, how was your sex life?

A. The sex was alright when she wasn't having physical problems and stuff. The sex life was okay.

Q. Was there any violent or aggressive behavior either on her part or on your part?

A. Yes on her part. She was...

Q. Alright, what happened?

A. She would have these in the closet violent streaks, like being upset with her family or... and taking it out on me. Like in public, she was you know like when you get older you know how to edit yourself and she wasn't very good at that. And I didn't want to put up with it man, and it was a lot of other little stuff going on here and there. And I would have moments when I would just go silent, wouldn't say anything to her and wouldn't give her sex and everything like that. And on a scale of 1 to 10 she was like a 6, 6 and a half. She had a bangin body, average face, shoulder length hair. Light skin, real big eyes and full lips. She was about 5' 5" I mean she was in shape. But she had this illness, a platelet count disorder with her blood and it would have her down in the dumps and I wouldn't treat her badly but I felt like sometimes she

SEVEN M.

would use her illness to hold me. So I talked to her about it and everything and she didn't want me to leave. There were many other small things that I didn't like about her and didn't like about myself when I was with her and I made her see those things. I have a way of showing a woman without belittling her or demeaning her. You know how she is to me and how I am to her. Anyway, one day I was coming home from work and she had got home before me and had started doing some hair in the kitchen. I had talked to her about this, and I counted in my own head; (I would never mention how many times even in our worst argument) I had told her about 19 times to stop leaving hair on the damn stove. I never addressed it by say in "the damn stove" but I said it to her. So she has five ladies in the kitchen, my food is cooked but there is hair, big globs of hair, fake hair all over the stove and there was even fresh packs of it. And their coats and stuff were everywhere even on the floor. So I said "hey ladies, how ya'll doing?" I made sure I was polite; made sure I watched my tone and all that. Not that I had a problem before, but I know she was hot-headed in the closet and I would have to deal with the consequences after they left. So I called her in the bedroom, real polite and everything and she came in there and was like "look, don't ask me to move no damn hair!" And I'm like whoa! You comin off all defensive and now I'm thinking, where are my keys? She had already snatched them, brought them in the bedroom and put them on the dresser and when I reached for them, she bit me on the hand. Now my man was with me and had a camcorder and had walked from the door to the kitchen and had started filming. He recorded us arguing and the women talking about what they were going to do. He's walking toward the bathroom and three of the women are right there and one of them had got one of my kitchen knives and they were all standing outside of the bedroom door talking about how they were going to kill me and this stuff like that. And I said, I don't need a relationship like this. Now my man that was there realized that he had now seen the stuff that I am going through. So I left, went outside with no warning. Didn't say I was getting them out my house or nothing like that. As I walked out, I had decided to slowly walk out and I said to myself that if her girlfriend is going to stab me, at least I could have some dignity. But I should have been smarter than that. I should've left earlier than that. So I went outside and called the cops and they got all of 'em outside and they wanted to know if I was gonna press charges because I showed the police the video. I showed where I said I was "callin the cops" in the video where my boy was filmin' me. This way, they would know why she hadn't called the cops, because she was being violent towards me. Plus she was allowing her girlfriends to threaten me and then she picked up a knife. I'm like; I know I didn't provoke this. I didn't threaten anyone, I mean, I did everything right. I thought at least. It was as if she had talked to them and convinced them of something otherwise obviously. I left everything I owned. Fur coats, flat screens...! left everything that I owned, my furniture- my new furniture. I left everything, just to leave her. And that was the end of that relationship. We called each other a couple times after that because I wanted to see how she was doing physically because I liked her as a friend on some level. And I uh, helped her pay her car off, I paid her car note, got that out the way. And it was a lot of small shit that no man would put up with. But I did it to give myself some longevity. To see what I could and could not deal with instead of running in a relationship. So I learned some things about myself. I guess that's pretty cool. I can only be who I'm going to be.

I don't believe in violence towards a woman or hurting a woman, or thought about doing anything wrong to them but when I tell you they make me sick; they piss me off. And I make them sick and we piss each other off... there are things we can do to make things better. I don't want to be in a violent relationship or one where I don't like myself in the relationship. I try to give, know when to say no, know when to say yes. To be attentive and very affectionate thru-in and throughout. No exaggerations on that. But I used to get sick of a woman falling in love with my dick and didn't love me as a person. I was too boring or too bland or I wasn't radical enough. So then I became harder towards women. There are three things that I won't tolerate. One is violence, public scenes is the other, and the other is, I simply wasn't attracted to her. So I'm not succumbing or settling for a woman anymore. I'm going to go after what I want because I can get it, and that's what it is.

Q: Were either of you in love?

A: She said she was in love and I told her that I loved things about her. That's the way I put it to her. That I was in love with the person she is, and that's the way I told her. And that was the beginning.

Q: The beginning?

A: That was the beginning of the relationship.

Q: One last question. When did you realize you were in a "situation?"

A: I realized I was in a situation when... I believed that I wasn't happy inside my heart and in my mind and I expressed that to her. I told her the one hundred percent truth. That I didn't like who I was in the relationship; that I didn't like who she was. She had more to offer someone else who could accept certain things about her and I could have someone who accepts certain things about me. And I said that I wasn't happy in this situation and it was time to get out.

Q: How long were you together when you realized that?

A: Around sixteen months. We separated in nineteen months.

Q: How did you get out?

A: I have a way of letting a woman know how to see herself. And she agreed that we need to be apart, but it was all verbal. She kept calling me, calling me, calling me and I kept trying to avoid her, then she just eventually stopped after about six months. She finally realized that that was it.

Q: Here's the big one. What would you do different?

A: Learn more about myself. Have more compassion for other people's feelings. I realized that telling the truth at the wrong time can cause more chaotic states than telling them at the right time. So it's like picking and choosing and learning from my mistakes. And showing love and respect for other people's feelings and realizing that being there mentally is different from being there physically.

Chapter 3

The Story of Crazy Mary

It was mid-October; my son and I were coming from a photo shoot downtown by Bleecker Street. So I took the opportunity to walk my young son around and show him what Bleecker Street and the area had to offer. I walked him past Fourth Avenue. I walked him past the Pink Pussy Cat Theatre and the IFC Theatre. I walked him past the Village Vanguard, Cafe Wha and all the little shops in between. We had fun. We looked at a couple of different spots. Me and my son, we're like best friends, it's a beautiful thing. Anyway, he is a pretty successful New York model and anytime we get downtown I like to show him the architecture, to make sure he doesn't miss anything because I am a real New Yorker. See I'm from Harlem. Harlem born, Harlem breed. I am also one of the most recognized faces in Harlem. See in Harlem in the 80's, it wasn't your name that was important, it was your face. People remembered your face and your face was like a coupon. Some coupons were more valuable than others. As far as that's concerned, I did okay in Harlem. And all the guys with the recognizable faces recognized the other guys with the recognizable faces. So this is where the story begins.

My son and I were walking past the shop downtown by Pizzeria Uno, looking at some bubble gooses in the window and I happened to spot someone from my old neighborhood in Harlem. He was a former model, one of those faces in Harlem everyone recognized. There were rumors, controversy, talk about gay shit. I was never exposed to it myself; whenever I was around him he was cool as hell so I had no qualms about introducing him to my son. My son is 6'2" weighs about 185 pounds and was 15 years old at the time. Now just for saying sake, for the purpose of keeping the story fluid without naming names we're gonna call this brother "Batman."

Now my son and "Batman" hit it off right away. My son is very witty; a slick talker like myself and so is this brother. A whole lot of Harlem testosterone firing in three different directions with sparks and glitter and shit. Yeah, I know, sounds crazy right? But it's some Harlem shit. Anyway, after we talked for a few minutes, we exchanged telephone numbers and asked about each other's families. I asked him how his sisters were doing, didn't think anything about it. Asked him about how his brothers were doing, didn't think anything about it and we parted ways. Now my son and I continued about our day, showing him the area, showing him the park and then we got back to the car. Shot back across the Lincoln Tunnel and we didn't think about this cat that we ran into "Batman" from Harlem, until the phone rang that night and it was his sister. Now I didn't even remember her name, I mean I had rode in the back of a jeep and she was in the front seat once for about 15 minutes but I didn't know this chick. I didn't know anything about her. I guess she was kinda cute, I mean she was cute enough for my boy, but that was 20 something years ago. So anyway I took the call, and we talked for about an hour that first time and I don't know, it was something strange about the conversation. Since I wasn't interested in getting into any type of relationship, I really didn't go way out of my way to share any type of witty banter or personal stories or speak the names of my family members to her. I wasn't trying to build that level of familiarity. I had just got out of a long term relationship and I really wasn't interested in any type of relationship. We talked on the phone and she seemed cool on the phone but... I don't know. We didn't speak the same language. We didn't care about the same things and she spent a lot of time on space book. Hours and hours and I am the opposite of that. I gotta live life, I gotta breathe the air, taste the air, smell the air, SHIT moves the air. I can't be plugged into the Internet for six, seven hours after I get off work. Still, I don't know, there was something harmless about her. So I said what the hell, she called me back, I took the call again. And we mostly talked about shit that happened in Harlem back in the days, and the people that we knew in common. It was cool but there was no connection, no chemistry, and no spark. I figured I wasn't in any danger and she seemed to be level headed so what the hell? She asked me to call her back, I called her back. Now, at this point "Batman" is setting up dinner at his family's house in Harlem. He calls me up and says- "hey why don't you come over, I'm cooking. I was just telling my people about you. How you're a stand up dude and how solid your reputation is in Harlem. I accepted those compliments and I believed that he was sincere when he made those compliments. I believed he knew from his heart and in the pit of his stomach that what he said to me was true and that what he was feeling was real. I mean I had worked hard to have the proper reputation. I walked away from a home, just gave it up, and signed it away, just to keep my reputation in tack. Like I said we respected each other so when he invited me out I said- "alright cool, I have this party I have to go to later on, so I will come through." I figured I would run over to Harlem real quick, holla at my man, I'll eat dinner with him, meet his people, say hi to his sister, if she shows up and that's it. But then when I get there, the house was beautiful man, it was beautiful, it was a beautiful place, you know what I mean? Somehow I ended up feeling like it was an ambush. I felt like I had gotten ambushed, because after we starting eating, Batman left.

The chick he was married to left. Everybody left and they left us downstairs. I finished eating and I am looking at her and like I said, I had seen her 20 something years prior and I thought she was kinda cute. But even then, she wasn't my type. I mean she was cool people but people want what they want. People like what they like, and they don't like what we don't like. Still, she seemed cool. She seemed like a good person. And I didn't mind being around her, even when she got aggressive. We were left alone, I'm sitting in a chair, she came over straddled me and started talking to me. I was like listen, we're gonna have to slow down cause I am not interested in any type of relationship. I don't even know that I am physically compatible with you and she was like- "nah nobody said all of that and you might change your mind." That kind of talk it didn't scared me. I mean I didn't know enough at that time to be scared, I didn't know enough. Red flags, alarms and signs man, I wasn't worried about that. I thought I was so BIG that I couldn't be harmed by some else's thoughts or intents. Man was I wrong man, really wrong. In any case, she tells me- "I know I have gained weight since the last time you saw me. That was a long time ago. You're in great shape, what are you doing are you a trainer or something like that?" I said yeah. So I starting going up and we picked out a treadmill and I started training her and showing her how to cook food and spending time with her daughter and making sure her daughter was eating right. I'm driving from where I am way up to where they are. I mean it's like 30 something miles man I'm cooking dinner, I'm bringing dinner, I'm going to the supermarket, I'm cleaning the kitchen, I mean washing dishes, you know what I mean, it's crazy how much shit I was doing in that house. Hold on a sec though, I'm getting ahead of myself. Remember when I was telling you remember when I was saying that when I saw her again at Batman's house, her brother's house, that I was on my way to a party? Well dig it I went to that party after I left there, and at that party I got into a melee. I'm surrounded by five mother fuckers, a couple of punches get thrown, I miss, somebody connects-catches me, and then they all run out the door. Meantime the cats I am with are asking me what happened and they were right there. That's a whole other story but, the deal is, the way I responded to what happened made me feel like maybe I shouldn't be around my crib for a couple of weeks, maybe I should lay low because the kangaroos, polar bears all types of animals was looking for me. So I chose to take this time to hide out somewhere else. And that's where shit got thick.

This is when I am going there. I'm cooking, I'm cleaning because I am hiding out at this chick's house, I am hiding out at my man's house in Harlem. But the one thing I am not doing is going to my own house. This is one of things that I have to take responsibility for. Because while I am hiding out, the woman in the house is getting the wrong idea. She is painting pictures in her head that are different from the pictures I'm painting in mine. I am not thinking about a future with her and I tell her this three times a day just to make sure that it does not get confused. Bet you can't guess what happened...shit got confused. So again, here I am hiding out. Now I want to reiterate, she was cool and there was really nothing wrong with her, but she wasn't my type. I'm absolutely sure that there was no future and again, I told her three times a day just to make sure shit didn't get confused. She tried to give me a key the first time I spent the night there, I refused. She asked me to sleep in the bed, I refused and I slept on the couch. In 45 days I must have spent 8 or 9 nights total at her house at her house and we made a couple of attempts at some type of intimacy or some sexual connection, but of course there was none. I just wasn't attracted to her. She just wasn't my type and this is the first rule that I broke. Never agree to be intimate with a woman that you are not attracted to. If this is not a woman that you're planning to be with, then keep your dick to yourself. It will only cause you problems. It doesn't matter if you're the clearest communicator in the world. It doesn't matter if your detection unit is broken or working at optimum speed. It doesn't matter if she agrees, looks you in the eye with the most grown up face possible and says yes, I understand, this will be about sex. This will be about something physical; this will be about the satisfaction of a human need without connection, consequences or confusion. None of that shit matters, not even in the least. None of it matters. The bottom line is, that's rule #1. Keep your dick to yourself, if all you have for this woman is a friendship and no future. Now I mean initially, when she approached me about being physical, it didn't sound like a good idea. I don't want to say something like I am repulsed or anything like that because again, this is not someone that I have some malicious feeling for. I don't hate this person, shit I don't even dislike this person. I understand how she got to where she got to. I know that someone as smart as I am, has to be responsible for what goes down. I am the sole controller of my universe. Shit, 9 times out of 10, 9 situations out of 10, I am the sole controller. But I am human, there are times when I don't say no firm enough, shit at least there was, not anymore. This shit here, this situation right here, has cured me. I have been stalked by women before. I had them chase my car down and buy me shit that I had to send back and attack my women and go through all types of shit. Changing their hair color. Switching from wiping from front to back, to wiping from back to front. They didn't give a fuck if they had a yeast infection, as long as they can be with me. I've been through that shit. I've been through it, but not like this. I was sure that I had covered every base. I was sure that I had communicated completely. I was sure that she understood. I was sure. But again I wasn't myself. I had been to war in the street countless times. Shot, stabbed, kidnapped. Even kidnapped by the feds once, but I still wasn't prepared. I wasn't prepared for this kind of focused, dedicated, negative, psycho, retarded, savant, bi polar crazy shit. I wasn't equipped for it. So at this juncture of the story, I have taken responsibility and I reiterate, keep your dick to yourself if you are supposed to be friends. It's not worth it. When she asked me to get involved with her physically, I explained to her, (laughs) I am not interested in any type of relationship and specifically not in a relationship with you. I just got out of a relationship with my safe sex partner. Now I know this is a term that most people are not hip to. It's my term, I own it. Library of congress knows that I own that. Now a safe sex partner is the most wonderful thing in the world especially in this climate, for grown people. This is an arrangement with someone that you agree and commit to have safe sex with. That you agree to show each other your doctor reports and checkups and that you report each other's tests and shit. The most important thing about having a safe sex partner is, once they agree the second date is at the doctor's office. HIV test, STD test, herpes, every damn thing possible. That is where the safe in safe sex partner comes from. Again it was the only position that was possible for me at that time. I am safe sex partner, no girlfriend, no boyfriend, no friend with privileges, no fuck buddies with benefits, none of that. Just friendship, so I broke rule #1. We'll get into rule #2 in a minute. Let's talk about why I fucked up and broke rule #1. No one else knew that I was hiding out except me and my people. No one else knew that I wasn't going home three four nights a week and staying at her house on the couch downstairs while she slept upstairs. No one knew that. No one knew that I had fallen in love with Mary's daughter. A pretty little girl, more pretty than cute. It was something special about her I had even fallen in love with the little boy upstairs. I even gave him a name and everyone around me knows that when I care about you I give you a name. If I haven't given you a name, then you are just not important to me. I felt like I knew that I was using her. Not for sex or for money or for her car like some grimy broke dude would, I showed up in my classic Porsche whenever I came. When I wasn't driving that, I pulled out the Audi twin-turbo just to bang around in. I didn't need anything from her except a place to hide out. I didn't need or want sex from her. I just needed a place to lay low. She couldn't cook, so there was nothing that she could do for me. Nothing. Only what I could do for her. Deep down I knew I was using her for a hide out, so I did everything that I could to absolve myself of feeling guilty about that. I cooked for her, I helped clean and on two separate occasions when she approached me for sex, I said yes instead of my customary no. The first time we had sex it was horrible and I told her so. She had jumped off the bed and rolled around on the floor screaming and just putting on. Elbows and knees and teeth and hair all over the place. No rhythm, not a rhythm I could catch anyway. The texture of the skin wasn't right. Again, I am not saying that she was unattractive or there was something wrong with her, but her skin texture wasn't right for me. The way she smelled wasn't right for me. We were not compatible at all. I never took my shirt off. It was all mechanical for me and I didn't try to fake like it wasn't. I operated like I was a maintenance man doing maintenance. She didn't even notice. She could have used a mechanical penis because she never looked, she never asked, she never talked to me. She just screamed a whole bunch of crazy shit, kicked me three four times bit me, and made me uncomfortable. I mean the shit was so horrible that after she had a couple of orgasms, I said oh okay that's it. That's it. And I hurried up, took a shower and ran downstairs, got on the couch and turned the television on both times. The second time, (I don't know what happened) there was blood everywhere. She had climbed on top of me and was jumping around and screaming, saying a whole bunch of crazy shit and here I am at half erection looking at her like she is fucking crazy. Somehow half of what I usually am was more than enough for her because again, she jumped off the bed, fell on the floor and rolled around like she was Patti La Belle at some fucking concert in 86. I just couldn't see it. There was no connection. There was no feeling and after the second time with the blood all over the place, I was sure that I would be exempt from all this. I didn't pull any punches. I used the word horrible; I said it was horrible for me. But I don't know, somehow it didn't reach her, somehow it didn't get through. Anyway, so I care about her as a person, not as a girlfriend ever, ever and every chance I got, I told her. I told anyone in her circle that would listen. But, it's a funny thing about people in your circle. Especially, when they have grown up with you. They know who you are, they know what your weaknesses are and any good friend or at least what most people would call a good friend is not gonna start digging into your psychology; into your emotional fucking problems every time you have a relationship failure. What they do is, clean you up, piece you back together and send you back out there to fuck up some more. This is what Mary's friends had been doing for her -her whole life. They know that there is something a little slow about Mary. They knew something was a little emotional unstable about Mary. Something mentally off about Mary, but they loved her and they still do. So if Mary cries foul, they jump on the band wagon. That's what they're supposed to do even if they don't have all the facts. That's what they're supposed to do. So I can respect their reaction. The fact is they're her people and there not going to expend the energy to check my record. To find out what my reputation is. To find out who I really am, so it makes no matter, talking to them would be a waste of time. Especially after shit was already fucked up. Here's this woman, I felt obligated to for the little bit of time I was there, I knew I was only going to be there for a couple of months. Long enough to get her training program together, to lose the weight that SHE asked ME to help her with. Long enough to get her nutrition plan together so her and her daughter can live happy healthy lives. To keep them away from diabetes so that they can have healthy pancreas and healthy livers and kidneys, I mean this is who I am. This is what I do. So I agreed to do it for her. In my mind, I knew her safe house that I was using and co habituating with her and her daughter and hanging out with the mother of the woman who lived upstairs I mean it was beautiful, I enjoyed it, and I loved it there. I didn't love Mary. But I loved being there. I loved being around these people.

It was cool. It was a family feeling in that house even though the apartment upstairs and downstairs were separated, there was a common entrance and the door was usually open. The mother of the woman who lived upstairs was a beautiful woman. In her sixties who loved to bake and cook and it had been so long since a woman had cooked me some food. Somehow this woman, Auntie Maggie sensed that I needed it and sensed that there was something beautiful and strong and safe about me and I sensed the same thing about her. She would bring me seafood salads when she knew I was there hiding out. She would bring me Chicken Parmesan, her own recipe, as if I was some exiled ruler who was thrown out of Harlem temporarily while there was some government takeover. She fed me, and Auntie Maggie came and talked to me. There were times that she talked to me at this point even before she knew I was just hiding out there. She treated me like I was her son. And there were times that we would talk about the old block on Third Avenue and the book that I wrote. And I felt like we were there. Like somehow, she was one of the grown-ups walking around while I was becoming who I was becoming. There were times that we sat and we talked and I was convinced that she loved me just like any mother would love her own son. So there was warmth there. And because I needed that at that time, I fucked up and I broke rule #2. We will get into that a little later.

So again, let me make sure that I'm painting the picture properly; I am playing housekeeper, cook and repairman. The repairman job was a steady job. You see this woman Mary had purchased one of these low income two family homes as an investment. The construction was horrible, there was no insulation in the floor or ceiling and you could hear the people upstairs having sex or talking or arguing or whatever the hell they were doing and as it turns out, they could hear us too. The walls were very thin and the construction materials weren't of the best quality. So there was always something to do, something leaking, some broken thermostat. Some mouse who had made its way into the kitchen behind the cabinets because of some gaping ass hole that the construction workers forgot to plug up. So there was always something for me to do. On the 8 or 9 times that I did spend the night there on the couch; she would leave me there and go to work. At this point, I had only been coming there through there 2 and a half weeks and this crazy ass broad Mary was talking about marrying me. Even though everyday, 3 times a day I took a drill and lobotomized this broad with the fact that there will never ever ever, ever, ever, ever be anything between us but friendship, she still went her own way. I never took her out anywhere, we never went to the movies, we never went to dinner. I mean I believed I was doing everything that I was supposed to do to keep things clear between us. I would never allow her to kiss me in the mouth, not even a peck. I would never allow her to call me anything but my name, and when one of her family members mentioned to me that somehow I was her boyfriend or something, I corrected them immediately. I mean the fact is her family and friends loved me. They met me, they felt the pure energy and they loved me. They knew that there was nothing wrong with me. The thing is, they thought I was an asshole in terms of the way I treated her, because they had the wrong impression. I mean if they had known that we were just friends they wouldn't have felt funny when I didn't let her kiss me in the mouth. If they had known that I wasn't her boyfriend and that I had been telling her that three times a day, then they wouldn't have felt funny when we walked into places and I didn't hold her hand. They wouldn't have felt funny when I didn't help her with her jacket. Or do all the polite things that a boyfriend or husband would do. On the other hand, because I loved the kids so much, I showed up to help out for a birthday party. I helped make cake and transport cupcakes and went to pick up her friend from the train station and brought her to the party with her child and (sighs) I shouldn't have done that. And why I did it was selfish. I wanted to have the connection with the kids; I wanted to be at the party. I wanted to enjoy that family setting you know I ...I was starting to long for that. I should have left long before. So anyway, every morning I would get up make myself something to eat, clean up, I'd track my business online. Make my phone calls, pay my bills and then I'd clean up and leave. There was one morning when

SEVEN M.

I realized my connection was becoming too powerful. That I was taking up too much space.

I woke up one morning and I was on the couch under the blanket with the television on low. This particular morning which was in actuality the last time I spent the night on that couch. Her daughter, her four year old daughter whom I'd come to love and who had come to adore me I hadn't seen her before I went to sleep. This particular morning, I wake up on the couch and I open my eyes and there's Mary standing over me.

Hair all over the place looking crazy, face dirty, looking like a fat nine year old girl with a bald spot. Just standing there staring at me like and I am wondering why is she standing there. And then I feel these small feet on the bottom of my feet and when I sit up I see her daughter on the other end of the couch covered up in a blanket. She was prone for waking up in the middle of the night and climbing into her mother's bed but that's not what she did this time, she came out of her bedroom, came downstairs and I don't' know, maybe she sensed I was there or maybe she heard the television and came down to see if I was there, but she decided that she would lay on the other end of that couch and sleep with me. And to me that meant a lot. As I sat up her little girl sat up too and as soon as she opened her eyes, she stared giggling. She and I, me and little girl shared a laugh and the acknowledgement of the friendship between us. I wasn't paying enough attention to see the look on her mother's face because Mary had gone deeper into her emotional psychosis. She had gone deeper into her hard of hearing, process shit the way I want to process it even though I heard it clean and clear shit, that's what she went into, she went into her crazy shit.her crazy Mary shit. But I can't blame her; I was the one fucking up. So anyway I get up that day and I cook breakfast, not the shit that microwave bullshit that she normally gives the baby I got up and I made the baby some oatmeal and some other stuff and we ate and it was at this time that the baby asked me if I was gonna come to her Christmas recital. Now believe me, believe me, all kinds of alarms and shit would have gone off if her mother had asked but it wasn't her mother asking, it was the baby and I had already decided that her mother had become too clingy and somehow she wasn't listening to what I was saying to her and even though two weeks had gone by and all the kangaroos and polar bears and animals who were looking for me (laughs) had already disappeared, or at least my mans in the street had disappeared them for me, I didn't have to be concerned anymore. I could have left at anytime and I had made the decision that that was too close and that waking up with the baby's feet on the bottom of my feet was too much. That no matter what I told this woman, I had to begin my exit strategy because she couldn't comprehend or listen anymore. That the words weren't making senses that somehow even my actions should have been colder. It was too warm. I didn't say NO hard enough, I wasn't firm enough, I really should have been. Anyway when the baby asked me to go to the Christmas recital I immediately agreed. I am a sucker for few things, small children who love me, cute old ladies and mean dogs. Ahhhh.. But the thing I am a sucker for the most-1 am the biggest sucker for a woman with tears in her eyes. Anyway the baby asked and I agreed. While I regret making certain decisions I can't say I regret that one. I am glad that I was there for the little girl, because it was about her. It was about her having a man to see when she came out the back and to ask what her performance was like and about her having me; this BIG giant dude who she thought so much of show up at her show and after the show I got in my car and left I went home. They went where they went and I felt good about that. Still I have to include the Christmas recital in one of the things I need to own that I did wrong, I actually shouldn't have gone. But now we are getting into rule #2. Now we remember that rule #1 is to keep your dick to yourself unless you're planning to be with the woman. Especially if you know that there is no future and NEVER EVER sleep with a woman that you are not attracted to. #1 keeps your dick to yourself. I think we've covered that. Now we get to rule #2. Rule # 2 is never ever, ever agree to go to a Christmas party, Christmas recital, but wait a minute let me let me back up, Christmas parties are cool, as long as everyone knows who you are, no scratch that, all parties are cool. Rule #2 you must never agree to go to any type of party that includes the family. If you show up at family events, friends and family will assume especially if the crazy broad that you're with wants that to be the assumption. If she wants them to assume that the two of you are together, then your dumb ass showing up at a family event, Christmas dinner at the house, Thanksgiving dinner, or birthday parties is a big fucking No No. This rule might be even more important than rule #1, because there are some women who you can look in the face and have an agreement with. But there are many women who would look you in the face and most of them agree to the terms and most of them believe they can stick to it. If your shit is a little bit bigger than average and you got some type of physical prowess or alpha male sexual power about you putting it all the way in is a big NO NO. But still that is part of rule #1 and as serious as rule #1 is it can't possibly compare to rule #2, so check this out, here is where I fucked that up. See I started hiding out at crazy Mary's house around November 15th- a week after we started hanging out or being friends or whatever; she had invited me to a Christmas party at her parents' house. Now since I knew I wasn't going to be around her anymore after the first part of the next year, I refused. I said- "you know I don't want to give them the wrong impression and I don't want to embarrass you because if anyone asks me if we are together I'm gonna tell them NO. I don't' want to embarrass you because I am getting the impression that you want more than that so I think that going to this family gathering and misrepresenting our situation would be a wrong idea." Smart right, intelligent right, practical right? Rational level headed talk right? Right! And what did she say in response? She agreed. She said okay, I don't think it will be like that and no one will get the wrong impression, it's just a Christmas party. I don't want to go by myself. I don't like my sister in law, my family is phony and they don't really like me, soooo I just wanted you to come with me. Damn....I mean ya know she had already shown a real fucked up pattern. I mean everyone that she introduced me to friends, family- whoever, she had something really fucked up to say, even about the woman upstairs. She had me believing that the woman upstairs had them coming and going, that she was fucking her baby's father's brother and still fucking her baby's father and fucking another dude that used to come in and out of there. Some pot head dude that she used to fuck with and she was fucking him and the milk man and the UPS man and that she was fucking somebody in the complex and that her best friend Tanya was the most opinionated big mouth bitch on the planet and that her sister was a dizzy broad who ran off to Atlanta with some down that used to cut her tires. I mean she talked so much shit, she talked shit about her brother Batman really is gay and she talked shit about her brother Ronald. That Ronald doesn't pay his own bills and she gotta pay his bills and that his wife Lenora doesn't love him and that she's fucking with some dude that she grew up. She talked shit about her other brother Dan and that Dan had a wife who was sneaking around and didn't like her and she stole her hats I mean she had so much gossip and negative shit to say about her family that I talked to her about it on three separate occasions. I said listen, we can't even be friends if you don't show loyalty to your family because if you talk shit about them, what will you say about me? Anyway, I started to think about what she was saying that her family didn't like her. Her father didn't care about her and her gay brother Batman had never been to her house even though she had owned the place for a year. It sounded sad and it wasn't the first time that I had played escort for someone, looked good, I'm in my early 40's at this time and shit I looked like most 30 year olds would like to look. I am in relatively good shape, 6 feet tall no stomach. My pipe game is official, and I am happy to say, I'm not lacking in certain areas. Its part of my man shit. It's part of being black. We're known for big dicks and ass whippings, the world over. I'm proud to be of the elite top of the food chain type of cats who fit into that category. So, would it kill me to go to this party and make her look good? No. But I made it very clear to her, after saying no to her the first four times she asked me, when she cried I made it very clear to her that I am gonna do this for you, but understand that if anyone asks me anything about a relationship, I am going to tell them the truth. And as she had done previous occasions, when we had grown up conversations, she agreed. This was a big mistake. When I got the party, the people in the house fell in love with me, and they fell in love with my son, who I brought along to make sure, again, that there would be no confusion. It was nice being there, in that family home, the place was beautiful. The food was beautiful, again that feeling of family, that I longed for, was there. I was able to talk with Batman and her brother Ronald, and her brother Dan, and to talk with her stepfather, and her mother who I had seen 20 year prior, who I still thought was an attractive woman, I thought her step father was one of the coolest black dudes I ever seen before, and I still do. I didn't think that her mother and she had a proper connection. There was some kind of disconnect there in terms of the connection between her and her other family members, but still it looked like family. And it felt good to me and I enjoyed it.

But still I shouldn't have been there. Even when her brother Ronald's wife Lenora who seemed to have known me from Jersey, she knew some of the same people I knew, When she referred to crazy Mary as my mate, I simply told her no no no no, not mate, friends. Even that wasn't enough to keep shit in order, to keep shit straight. Cause the fact is her family didn't want to hear anything like friends. They didn't want to hear that we weren't together.

Shit, they wanted her to have something to do. They wanted her to stay the fuck out of their hair. No one cared to talk to me to tell me she was out of her fucking mind. That she had issues. No one talked to me. They were just happy to have me around so she could have what it is that entertained her. And that's fine, they loved her and I guess they still do, but again, there was a disconnect, didn't feel right. So anyway, after she played family with everyone except Darien's wife, for whom she openly showed contempt, we left in our separate cars. Her daughter in the back seat of her car, my son in the front seat of mine and she had her blue tooth on and I had my speaker phone on and we were talking and she went into straight talking shit about her family. She talked spot and I hung the phone up on her and I didn't speak to her anymore that day or the day after I was so tired of running her friends down to me ya know acting like they weren't shit and that they were all against her and was some conspiratory bullshit. She even called me one day crying, talking about her father told her that she needed to get her teeth cleaned. I mean screaming and fucking crying. Someone at work asked her if she was pregnant and she hadn't been pregnant in five years. She didn't take these cues to get her mouth cleaned, get her teeth fixed or to lose weight. She saw this as people attacking her trying to do harm. Her problems were deeper than anything I could possibly help her with. I mean I am not her fucking therapist; I had my own shit to deal with. Bottom line is, my showing up at that Christmas party wasn't smart because again, it made things worse. It made her people think we were together regardless of what I was saying. She was telling them something different than I was telling them and they believed her. Why the fuck would they not? No here's what so fucked up about rule #2. Even after the Christmas party I gave my word to myself and I would never put myself in a situation like that again, but here's what's fucked up. On my way into the Christmas party at her family's house, I gave my word that I would show up and at her birthday party. It was supposed to be at some club downtown on 45th Street. One of her friend's husband, was a half ass fledgling promoter whose parties only the hood rats and dead beat ass niggas from Mount Vernon and friends and family would show up to support. I mean know he is no P Diddy, ya know, what the fuck ever. So I decided to say fuck it that I would show up at this birthday party. That I would I would exchange gifts that I had already ordered when I thought we were just going to be friends. Shit I had already ordered this shit and agreed to this shit before I knew I was gonna have to listen to this permanently. Now at this particular event I broke two rules, I broke rule #1 again and broke rule #2. See my dumb ass; my problem is I'm very intelligent so I can rationalize shit and say fuck it. I show up at one more thing, let this crazy bitch see my dick on more time and then I am out of here for good. I'm outta here for good. I got her to get on a fucking tread mill. I got her to buy one, try to eat right, get some diet books, I did all I could fucking do. I was ready to get the fuck outta there man. Fuck it! And although I had fallen in love with the little girl and the little boy upstairs, I was willing to give those relationships up.

Shit I still had contact with Aunt Maggie. So I was alright in that area.

Shit at least I could check on the little boy upstairs. But I was ready to go, so I figured Fuck It. I'd go for broke. Anyway, fast forward to January. It's the end of January, my birthday was the first week of February, this crazy broad Mary's birthday was the last week of January, and her daughter's birthday was the last week of January as well. So, like I was saying, I mean to come to and help at her daughter's party ya know and ah help her celebrate hers to represent her as a happy, whole person for her birthday before I broke the fuck out. Anyway, fast forward. We go to this party at this place called Montell's downtown Manhattan, again organized by her friend's husband, the fledgling half ass promoter. So I get dressed. I had another engagement before that; a meeting. So I get dressed; she called me five, six, seven times. Still asking, are you still coming are you still coming, and I of course say yes because I agreed to come. Now I know the party started at 10 o'clock and I knew it was going to be over at 4am. But I didn't show up to meet her til almost 12 o'clock. I went to her job and picked her up and we rolled the seven blocks to the party.

I parked the car and as we we're getting out, I got her birthday present. It was a watch. We he had agreed back in November that although I don't exchange birthday I mean Christmas presents that I am a big fan of giving birthday gifts even to friends. So she said I want a watch, I said fine and she knew that I liked them and she said she would get me one- and that was that. Neither of the watches where over a couple of hundred dollars so, it was an easy gift and since it didn't cost much it was fine. Got her a few balloons (because it was her birthday) so she could look festive walking into her own party and that was it. I knew that all I had to do was go through 15 or 20 minutes of her jumping up and down on me and then it would be over with forever. So I just wanted to get through the night. Shit. I was half smoked up when I got there man.

I had to stop and get something to smoke. I was high as hell when I went to meet her. I walked in the party and I just found a corner and leaned up. I never took my sunglasses my jacket or my scarf off the whole time I was there. There was a DJ that I knew, who had been operating in Harlem for about 25 years and he knew her and he knew everyone else at the party.

When he saw me, he immediately called me by my old street name Fat Cat. What's happening, Fat Cat. I said what's up.

He's like what you doing here? And I told him I'm here with Mary, on her night. He was like "oh escort huhh, lucky for her." I said "how bout that." That wasn't the only conversation that went that way that night. I mean I had spoken to two other people and I had to let them know what was going on. At this point I was so uncomfortable about was happening, I went back to my corner and leaned up. Her sister in law Lenora was taking pictures of me from across the room and I started to feel uncomfortable so I thought-let me go to the bar to get something to drink. At this point Mary comes back from wherever she is. As she walks up, there is a guy following her. He's got a three piece suit on. A funny looking little dude. Anyway, he walks up and he's staring at me and staring at her like she is the most beautiful woman in the world. Now in the morning she reminds me most of Shrek from the movie, but shit, there someone for everyone I guess, and this dude was looking at her like she was a bag of thousand dollar bills. Anyway so we walk over to the bar, and we when we got to the bar, we see her friend Tanya. When Tanya sees the box she carrying, Tanya grabs the box opens it, sees the watch, puts her arm around me and starts hugging me. Now when I pull back from her and put my elbow between us she says

"I'm sorry, am I making you uncomfortable" and my response was "no... No... I'm not uncomfortable because I am hiding my penis behind your friend." Now I know from the outside looking in that might sound like an arrogant asshole type of something to say but if you knew if I didn't want to be there and if you knew that I wasn't this persons boyfriend and you knew that her hugging me is sending the wrong message because you got this warm fuzzy feeling that she's finally got someone to buy her a watch and treat her good and unh unh - you had the wrong fucking impression. And if you knew what was going on, you would have understood, she would have understood my statement the way I made it. I was just trying to get through the night. So as we walk back to my table and I lean up again, the same funny looking dude is standing there.

With this strange smile on his face, looking at me and I felt uncomfortable. I thought he was some type of homo or something, but ya know; shit its okay to be homosexual. So I didn't think too much of it, I didn't make a big deal out of it. I kept doing what I was doing. So I'm standing there and I am having the most miserable time of my life and I'm just waiting for the night to be over. I asked her if she was ready to go so we could get the rest of the fucking up night over with man, so I could wake up the next day and move on. And never be in this situation again. Never never put myself, my reputation, my dick, or my face on the line in a situation that I could never see myself in. So as I am standing there, she comes over and she tells me about the guy, the little goofy guy named Avon. Now he was a goofy little dude and I don't know somehow when she walked past him and they spoke I thought they looked cute together, and I said so. I suggested that she should pursue that. I was talking about how she should pursue this guy named Avon. She had been involved in some type of oral sexual act with him and they seemed to like each other but I don't' know what happened. Since all I was trying to do was get a clean exit strategy going, shit I talked that nigga to death. I talked about him when we went to go to my car, saying bye to her friends, I told her she better go say by to Avon. When we got out to the car,

I said ya know that guy Avon seems to like you a lot and like I said, I kept telling her that they looked cute together and that she should pursue that since this is our last night hanging out. I thought that maybe she could pursue someone who genuinely likes her and I am telling her, "Why would you turn your back on all that, that's so hard to find."

But of course she wasn't listening to me. Shit, she thought she was smarter than me. She thought I was just talking. That someone how I was just bluffing and I wasn't as firm in my convictions as I was. That this may not be the last night that she sees me. But I knew different. I knew for sure that this was it. That I would never take my clothes off with this person again, or show up at a birthday party, Christmas recital for her daughter or any other event, at all. Ever. That I was done punishing myself for using her home as a safe house for two weeks. That I was finished paying for anything that I felt like a person should pay for to be in the same space as someone while their hiding from some other situation. I had finished paying for everything. Shit I had more important things on my mind anyway, It was like an out of body experience, that night for the most part cause I wasn't even there, I was more concerned with an investment I had just made with my mother who had been dealing in real estate on and off for years. So anyway, I end up at the hotel with this woman after leaving club Montell's and again-a horrible physical experience! I was so happy that it was over that I sat up in the bed smiling and she's on the floor writhing around and carryin on and I just sat there smiling. I couldn't stop smiling because I knew that this was the last time. The last time I would have nails, teeth and elbows in my groin. The last time I would have to fight with this person who had no rhythm at all. Not in a bed, a car, a club or in life. I just kept smiling. I don't know what she was thinking about, maybe she thought I had liked what just went down, but all I knew was this was it. I would never have to give my word to this person for anything ever again. When she sat up, she started talking about how she wanted to rescind our agreement about this being the last time, I said hell no! When I said no, she started to cry. Funny thing is, while she was crying, the dude Avon called her. He was calling to tell her that he was thinking about her and how handsome he thought her escort was; which I thought was some homo shit anyway because now, I'm thinking about how he was standing there looking at me with that goofy look on his face. And I told her, this guy really likes you. He really likes you. You really should pursue that. She didn't take that well, but at that point; I really didn't give a fuck.

Now we move onto rule #3. Never, ever mix money with a woman! Like I said, I was in the middle of investing money with Ms Eartha on a property in SC. I had about 4300 on stash and since I was gonna get some money two weeks later I wasn't really worried about throwing it all up. I only had to pay half for the whole property like I said for 24 acres I was able to get 7500 not a bad deal at all. Now since and this chick and I were friends and I had been paying bills for her and helping her do things and I mean she helped me to do a lot of things too. I took her with us to pick up a classic Volkswagen Beetle, she went with me out in Brooklyn to pick up some money, I mean she was turning out to be a good friend on the friend front but she wasn't really being my friend, her motivation was something else entirely. That's fine because we're all in relationships from time to time where a man would try to buy a woman or a woman may try to buy a man, as soon as she heard that I was making this investment, and I was on the phone complaining to my mother that I wasn't going to send her my last 43oo, I'll be broke for two weeks she hurried up and volunteered she said wait a min why don't you get the property and

I'll hold you down for the next two weeks, You can get some more money out of the street, I was like nah nah nah and I mean even though she asked this question, during the first three weeks we were hanging out I knew I wasn't going to be there my immediate reaction was no no no. But then she worked on me, she said listen think of it as a investment and if everything goes right when you sell the property ya know you just give me a good profit. So I mean, I am from Harlem man so buy low sell high that's in my blood. when she said that shit that sounded like some Harlem shit to me, I knew she had her head on tight so she was like what will it take to get you through the next two weeks I said 7 or 8 hundred so what does she do, I think she went to work and got the money or from an atm. Wherever she went, she got the money. She handed it to me and she said you know what, hold on to that and you can rock from there and I said fine. Now I am thinking to myself that this is some real grown up shit here, wrong, be that would later come to bite me in the ass that rule #3 never mix money with a woman your not going to be staying with, never mix money with a woman you are not married to and never mix money with a woman that you know your not going to be with. Shit, the bottom line is never mix money. I am so cured from this experience that when I get married next time, my money is going to be separate from my wife's money. I never ever, ever, ever want to be in that situation again. Anyhow, I had escaped that Montells situation, it was over. I had survived that horrible physical experience in the downtown hotel. It was over but it was the beginning of something else. Something I wasn't ready for. Some truly fucked up behavior. The kind of behavior that I could usually walk away from, but this situation I could not. I had become a tangible substitute for Spacebook six hours a night. I was something tangible and she didn't want to let go, but I was gonna make her let go. This is when the text messaging starts. In the six days after the Montells fiasco, six days after the horrible situation at the hotel was over finally, she sent me three hundred and five messages. That's over 60 text messages a day and she called me 105 times. In six days! That's over 15 calls a day! 305 text messages and they were all the same, in the morning they were always apologetic "Oh you are the greatest man ever, and I am so sorry for my behavior and for lying to my family about you and I'm sorry I lied to my friends". Then in the afternoon, she'd just get negative. She would wake up every morning, stretch, rested, and come to her senses and realize that she owed me an apology. Then in the afternoon when she felt lonely again, she would get negative. It was an incredible psychosis because she would wake up, apologize, and then in the afternoon she would hate me as if I had removed her heart and stomped all over it. She hated me because regardless of what I wanted, she wanted to be with me. It was all my fault. Then at night, when shit got dark and lonely, the messages would be about how she wanted to have sex with me and how she wanted to be with me. How she would do anything. I didn't respond to these messages. Then again, I didn't respond to most. Out of 305 messages, I must have answered fifteen. And my responses were all the same:" I'm sorry, just leave me alone." It got so bad, the crying and mood swing shit- and the texting all night long, that I started to worry about her health. I was concerned that she wasn't sleeping. That she wasn't eating.

She was a mess. So was I. I had no idea that this was going to be the reaction when it was time for me to go. Shit scared me so much, I set up a meeting with her brother so I could tell him that she's bi-polar. Unfortunately meeting and talking with Batman did me no good. Absolutely no good. Soon as I told her that I was going to talk to her brother and father, she started talking about how they don't care about her. And that they don't love her and that they never did. Again, I felt bad, but not bad enough to put myself back into that situation. So I tried another approach because she wouldn't stop calling me, she wouldn't stop texting me. I even made the local police aware of her license plate number and car make because I was genuinely concerned that I wouldn't be able to get rid of this woman. That hiding out in my own home with all the lights off wouldn't be enough. That turning off my phone and computer wouldn't be enough.

I made three mistakes.

I agreed to intimacy with a woman that I didn't want to be with.

I agreed to attend family events.

I even agreed to mix money with her.

The last of which was the worst because it was the thing that she misrepresented best to her friends. They had no idea that it was an investment that I'm still making money from now. After meeting with her, her brothers and receiving invoices for q- tips and gas; she sent me an invoice for muthafuckin Q-tips! H She asked me once on her way to my apartment if I needed anything and I said, Q-tips, and now she was saying I owed her for that. When it was all over with, she not only wanted the $800 investment money back, she wanted $500 in punitive damages and money back for a pair of socks and a belt that she bought my son. So I met with one brother on two occasions and gave him almost five hundred. I met with the other brother and gave him over five hundred and I gave her more than three hundred. Now, I don't know how your math is, or what kind of fuckin calculus expert you are but that's $1300. I had paid over $500 in extortion money and she still wanted more. I had done my best to make things easier for her when I was leaving. And she made things worse for me. Put me through months of hell unnecessarily. I paid the extortion money. And still ended up misrepresented in her small social circle. At the time, I didn't give a fuck. Those people weren't my friends. They weren't my family, they were hers. She didn't mean anything to me either. But, I miss the little boy upstairs, Aunt Maggie and I miss the little girl. And I was sorry that she had disrespected the privacy of her friend who lived upstairs. She was checking her phone records and invading her apt and all types of other crazy shit to make sure that she wasn't my friend. I apologize for any harm caused anyone during the course of Crazy Mary's shit.

Please be careful out there.

Chapter 4

The Worst

This last account is about myself, the author. When I was first asked to do this, I had no idea that the superior court would write part of this book for me. While I was finishing interviews and compiling research, I fell victim to a real female stalker. It is one of the greatest testaments to irony I have experienced as a writer. On the very night that I finished interviewing the subjects of this project, I became the victim of the most dangerous person of this work. In the spirit of transparency and truth, I have included the actual transcript from the court proceedings that followed my false arrest. By the time the hearing was over, they were trying to arrest her lying-ass.

Last year a story aired about a female doctor stole the sperm of her lover who was a male doctor. She convinced him to ejaculate in her mouth, ran into the bathroom to "spit". She spit alright, right into a syringe, inseminated herself, had the baby and hijacked him for $4000 a month in child support. When she was snitched on by a co-worker she had betrayed, the judge was not happy. She had made a fool of him, used the creation of a life to punish her doctor friend for not committing, and then used the court to rob, extort and damage the reputation of a well respected surgeon. The judge not only reduced the child support to $200 a week but he made her pay the doctor every cent that he paid before he reactivated the lower child support payment. The only reason he didn't lock her up was because of the very man that she wronged.

This story was aired on the Michael Baisden show. The ill shit is, same thing almost happened to me. Don't believe it, check it out. Not even I could make up some shit that good.

For the two women who sat in the gallery with me. The ones who are legitimate victims of domestic violence. The same ones who clapped and cheered for me when the truth came out. To the ones who would never fabricate a story to harm someone when they want to end or modify their relationship. I wish you justice.

To the bullies who use violence to control those who are weaker than them, and the liars who use the court room to wage war against their ex-best friends, please stay away from me. I'm not trying to threaten you and it's not that I hate you, but I think that it would better for everyone if you were not around.

SEVEN M.

SUPERIOR COURT OF NEW
JERSEY BERGEN COUNTY
CHANCERY DIVISION,
FAMILY
PART DOCKET NO.:
A. D. #

Plaintiff,

vs.

TRANSCRIPT
OF
HEARING

SEVEN MUHAMMAD,
Defendant.

Place:

Date: March 8, 2011

BEFORE:

TRANSCRIPT ORDERED BY:

MR. SEVEN MUHAMMAD

APPEARANCES:

} M J A . Pro Se

MR. SEVEN MUHAMMAD, Pro Se Defendant

Audio Recorded Recording

Opr: Unknown

SURVIVING A FEMALE STALKER

Colloquy

THE COURT: The docket number is

FV-02-1829-11. I'm going to swear both of you in.

THE CLERK: Would both of you please raise your right hand.

PLAINTIFF, SWORN

SEVEN MUHAMMAD, DEFENDANT, SWORN

THE CLERK: You can put your arms down. Ma'am, starting with you

please state your full name and spell your last name for the record.

MS. [][][][][][][][]:

THE CLERK: And you, sir, likewise.

MR. MUHAMMAD: Seven Muhammad, last name M-U-H-A-M-M-

A-D.

THE CLERK: Thank you, sir.

THE COURT: Okay. You may be seated. Ms. you obtained a

temporary restraining order regarding, against Mr. Muhammad.

MS. [][][][][][][][]: Yes.

THE COURT: That's funny. «, On March 1st?

MS . [][][][][][][][]: March   —

THE COURT: Relating to a January incident?

MS. [][][][][][][][]: Yes. I've didn't report it then and there, but I

reported it after.

THE COURT: What took you so long?

SEVEN M.

Comments by Ms . [][][][][][][]

MS . [][][][][][][][]: I didn't know. I. thought it would just go away.

THE COURT: Okay. Did it?

MS. [][][][][][][][]: That it would just, it did, but he's unpredictable. So I.cion't know. I don't want him to contact me or anything. And I'm pregnant, so I didn't want --

THE COURT: Well did he, with his child?

MS. [][][][][][][][]: uh-huh.

THE COURT: Well don't you think you're going to have contact?

'   v "

MS. [][][][][][][][]: No. There's no contact after what he did.

THE COURT: Well what do you think Mr. Muhammad is going to want to do when you deliver his child?

MS. [][][][][][][][]: He told me he doesn't want anything to do with the child.

THE COURT: Well how, are you going to need support?

MS. [][][][][][][][]: Yes. I'm going to get support.

THE COURT: Right.

MS. [][][][][][][][]: But as far as contact during that time, no. And I didn't want him contacting me months down the line saying anything.

THE COURT: Well you don't really, if Mr. Muhammad comes to court and wants to see your child, it's going to beAthe court's decision.

MS. [][][][][][][][]: Oh, I understand that. But I wanted it on the record that he put his hands on me.

THE COURT: Okay. But what took you, you waited —

MS. [][][][][][][][]: Because I didn't —

THE COURT: — two months.

MS. [][][][][][][][]: I did wait long. I did. I did wait long. - But I mean it wasn't, it wasn't right. And it's not

THE COURT: Did you know you were pregnant in January?

MS. [][][][][][][][]: Yes. I did.

THE COURT: All right. It is your, you want a final restraining order; right?

MS. [][][][][][][][]: Yes.

THE COURT: Okay. It is your burden to prove that an act of - .domestic violence occurred and that it's reasonable that you have a reasonable fear of the defendant.

MS. [][][][][][][][]: Uh-huh.

THE COURT: It's reasonable to enter a final restraining order in your favor. Do you understand that?

MS. [][][][][][][][]: Yes.

SEVEN M.

THE COURT: I don't have anything in my file but your complaint. I don't have any —

MS. [][][][][][][][]: Right.

THE COURT: — police reports. I don't have pictures. I don't have police officers at my disposal. Whatever evidence you need, voice mail messages, text messages, facebook pages, my space pages, pictures, witnesses, it's.up to you to bring them.

MS. [][][][][][][][]: Okay.

THE COURT: Okay. Are you prepared to try the case today? Because if we --

MS. [][][][][][][][]: I mean I only have pictures on my phone.

THE COURT: -- if we begin the trial, and I'm not going to tell you how to try a case. You have the right to certainly speak with an attorney or hire an attorney. Okay. And sometimes ADV can appoint an attorney at no cost to you. But it's sometimes to get one very quickly. Are you prepared to proceed today with all the evidence you need, because if we start the trial, we'll finish the trial.

MS. [][][][][][][][]: I only have pictures on my phone. They're not printed out. And I don't —

THE COURT: Pictures on your phone are fine.

MS. [][][][][][][][]: Oh, okay.

THE COURT: Do you have sufficient evidence to prove the case?

MS. [][][][][][][][]: Yes. Pictures on my phone, that's it. I mean I can't say that, I mean no one is going to say oh, it was him who did it. Or no one was there. It was just me and him.

THE COURT: Okay. So you want to try the case today?

MS. [][][][][][][][]: No. No, because I mean, I'm trying to see like if I show the pictures on my phone I can't prove that he's the one who did it. They could say someone else did it arrd not him.

THE COURT: Well it's up to you. That's a matter of credibility. Do you need time to prepare more evidence?

MS. [][][][][][][][]: No. We can try it today.

THE COURT: Okay. Mr. Muhammad, did you get a copy of the restraining order?

MR. MUHAMMAD: Yes, I did, Your Honor.

THE COURT: Okay. When were you served with that?

MR. MUHAMMAD: I was served with the order less than 10 days ago.

THE COURT: Okay. Did you have a chance to read it?

MR. MUHAMMAD: Absolutely.

THE COURT: Okay. The consequences of a final restraining order? re significant. And I'd like you to listen very closely.

If I find that you committed an act of domestic violence and it's reasonable to enter a final restraining order to protect the life, safety, or well being of the plaintiff, your name will be included in a registry. ,

SEVEN M.

There are agencies that have access to those names and it may cause you problems in the future. Getting a professional license, getting a job, people are detained in airports, among other things. Okay.

You will be fined between $50 and $500, and that's at my discretion. You will not be allowed to possess weapons and you will be fingerprinted immediately following the hearing. Do you understand all that?

MR. MUHAMMAD: I absolutely do.

THE COURT: Okay. This is a civil matter.

It's in the family court. So you don't have a right to a public defender. You certainly have a right to hire a lawyer or speak to a lawyer. And if you need time to do that I will give you time to do that. Okay.

In the meantime there's to be no contact between you and the plaintiff. If you violate that no contact order it becomes criminal contempt. Okay.

If you're found guilty twice of criminal contempt of a restraining order there's mandatory incarceration of 30 days. Do you understand that?

MR. MUHAMMAD: I absolutely do.

THE COURT: Okay. Are you prepared to proceed today or do you need an adjournment?

MR. MUHAMMAD: I am absolutely ready right now.

THE COURT: Okay. Do you have any witnesses in the room?

MS [][][][][][][][]: No. It's just us.

THE COURT: Do you have any witnesses in the room?

MR. MUHAMMAD: Absolutely no witnesses.

SURVIVING A FEMALE STALKER

THE COURT: Okay. Okay. Ms. [][][][][][][][] you can proceed.

MS. [][][][][][][][]: Okay. On January 5, well the week before January 5th I found out that I was pregnant along with the defendant. We took a pregnant test together. And we were, we spoke about it and I was aware of the fact that he didn't want anymore children.

And I wasn't ready myself, but, ma'am, I don't believe in abortion. And I was kind of scared.

It was a thought in my mind. So I did call the abortion clinic and I spoke with the defendant about that.

As it got closer, you know, time was, I was supposed to go to the clinic to go get it done. I called and then I called Mr. Muhammad and I said to him that I was kind of scared. So he said, no problem, just come talk to me, you know, whatever, we'll get through this together.

So I went to his house and I went there and I spoke to him and I said, you know, I'm not going to be able to do it.* I can't do it. I can't do that to my child. I already have a son and I just can't do it.

And he spoke for awhile and he was like how could you do this. And you know how I feel about having another child. And I was like, I-know, I said, but there's other options. Let's just give it up or let's just do, let's do something else. You know, it's going to be hard for me too, you know what I mean. And he was just like well you already knew that you weren't going to have an abortion. I said, no, I didn't know because I called. Even though I don't believe in it I was

52

SEVEN M.

thinking about my life too. But I realized I couldn't do it. And I informed him of
that.

He got upset. And he was like well you just need to go. So I was about
to leave his house. And when I was about to leave he started bringing up old
things in our relationship that I said it made no sense to talk about right then and
there.

But I said, okay, if you want to talk about it then you're going to take
responsibility for what happened with that situation. So we sat back down and I
sat down and he got very upset.

And I would like to get up and leave. I got to the door. At the door he
put his hands around my neck and he put me on the wall and was banging my
head on the wall.

Now when I moved from over there I went- to the couch and I asked
him to explain what just happened. I said you told me last week you would
never put your hands on me. You would never hurt me. Why did you, I said,
what did you just do. And I told him to explain it.

He said, I scratched him on his neck. Which I did scratch him because
after he went at my neck I went back at him -¬THE COURT: But you were by
the door?

MS. [][][][][][][][]: Yeah, I was by the door.

THE COURT: He grabbed you by the neck?

MS. [][][][][][][][]: Grabbed me by the neck.

THE COURT: He picked you up?

MS. [][][][][][][][]: Yes, on the wall.

THE COURT: And then you decide rather than exiting the door -¬MS. [][][][][][][][]: I couldn't exit.

THE COURT: No. But then you went back into the house.

MS. [][][][][][][][]: Because I was, after he let go of me I went this way (indicating). I couldn't reach back to open the door to leave.

THE COURT: Right. But you went back and sat down.

MS. [][][][][][][][]: Yeah. I went back towards the couch. Yes, I did. I went back towards the couch. THE COURT: Why didn't you walk out?

MS. [][][][][][][][]: I couldn't just walk out.

THE COURT: Why not?

MS. [][][][][][][][]: First of all he's never put his hands on me like that. So I was upset.

THE COURT: I understand that, but no, no, no. Right. But,. after it happened— MS [][][][][][][][]: uh-huh.

THE COURT: — why didn't you leave?

MS. [][][][][][][][]: I don't know. I didn't think to just run out-the door. And I was, I wanted him to explain. I was why did you do that. So I didn't just exit.

And*I went to the couch and I was like what did you, why did you do that. Why, I was like, don't touch me. Get away from me and I was moving.

THE COURT: And how were, what was your demeanor?

MS. [][][][][][][][]: What do you mean? If I was upset or scared?

SEVEN M.

THE COURT: Yes.

MS. [][][][][][][][]: I was scared.

THE COURT: You were scared but you went back in and sat down,

MS. [][][][][][][][]: But I didn't just sit down like that, Your Honor. I sat down. I was on the couch and he was in front of me and I was moving back like this. And I said I just want to leave. I just want to go home. Let .me just gp home. I just want to leave.

And he was like, no. We're going to talk.

THE COURT: But that doesn't, I'm a little confused.

THE COURT: You're by the door.

MS. [][][][][][][][]: I was by the door and that's where he —

THE COURT: You want to leave.

MS. [][][][][][][][]: Yes. But, I went —

THE COURT: So instead of leaving —

But the door wasn't open,

Your Honor. It was locked. It was not open.

THE COURT: Well how do you open it?

MS. [][][][][][][][]: Well I didn't turn back to open it. But he was there at the door. But I didn't, he never, I didn't think to leave.

THE COURT: But then you went down, sat on a couch, and said now I want to leave.

no, no, no. I didn't just go and sit on the couch. I went over to the couch. He followed me over to the couch, like he was right there. It's not like he stood by the door and watched me walk over to the couch. He was right by me.

And when I got on the couch he hovered over me and I was kind of pushing him away and I was like, let me just go, let me just go. Let me just go. And I was like, yo, you just put your hands on me. And I was upset and I was cursing at him- And then I was. Like, I just want to go. '• I just want to go.

And he was like, no, no, we're going to talk.

We're going to talk. I said, no. If you can't sit on your hands and talk to me then we have nothing to talk about. And I was like I just want to go. I just want to go.

Then he started talking about all types of other stuff. I sit down; he sits in between my legs and was in my face him away. I can't just push him away like that and run out. It's just me and him.

I didn't know what he was going to do. If he was going to drag me back in there. If I was going to make it to the door, if I was going to make it out. My phone is in my coat. I couldn't call anybody and do anything. 'v

So I was in there and we were arguing, arguing, arguing, so he kept putting his hands on me.

He kept, he kept touching me. He picked me up. The final stroke was when he picked me up and the window ended up breaking. And he slams me on the ground, put his knee in my neck.

SEVEN M.

And at that point he went, after that he was saying, come, come, let's go to the room. Let's go to the room. And. I was like I don't want to go to the room. THE COURT: What room?

THE COURT: Why?

*   Because I guess the window broke and I don't know if he thought people were going to hear us talking. Because he window broke very loudly.

We went to the room. I sat on the very edge of the bed. And I didn't look at him. I had my back to him. He was talking to me and he was like Nicole, just look at me, just look at me. Talk to me. He was like, talk to me.

Then he realized his shirt was ripped, my shirt was ripped.

THE COURT: How did his shirt get ripped?

MS. [][][][][][][]: From all the fighting, I guess. From all the fighting. Because my shirt was ripped as well. And then he went and got a wash cloth to wipe my face off. And I was like, no.

I went to the sink and I washed my own face.

And then at that point I seen my face and my neck and I screamed. And I said, why, at that point. Because I just couldn't believe that he did that me. We never had that kind. of relationship before. All because I wouldn't have an abortion.

All because we could have just sat down and talked about it. You don't do that. That's not how you resolve these things. We could have talked about. He could have feaid, look;

I don't want to have anything to do with you. That's it. I don't want to have anything to do with you. And, hey, I'll help you out. This is your decision, it's your body. I'll help you monthly. I can't be around the child at all. But that's what it is.

I would have took that better than his putting his hands on me.

THE COURT: Okay. So then what happened?

MS. ITIIBIITI: And then after that I left.

After that, no, after that -¬THE COURT: lid he stop you from leaving?

MS. [][][][][][][][]: That was the last. After, you know, wiping off my face he seen how my shirt was ripped. So he said, okay, change your shirt and change your shirt.

So I took my, so at that point I wasn't saying anything. I kind of shut down. I didn't say anything. I don't want to say anything else to piss him off. I didn't want to say anything. I just shut up.

So I took the shirt off. He gave me a shirt that had; it was a white shirt at first. And I guess I was about to leave and then he said, no, no, no, no. Change that. And he gave me a plain black t-shirt, which was just an ordinary shirt.

So I put on the ordinary shirt and then he was like, well, I didn't expect it to end like this.

And all of this. I just looked at him and I said uh- huh. And then he said, oh, well I forgive you. I forgive you for past incidents. And I looked at him and I was like, well, thank you.

SEVEN M.

And then we got to the door and he was like all right, bye Nicole. And I said bye Seven. And I left.

THE COURT: All right. This was on January 5th —

- [][][][][][][][]: This is January 5th.

THE COURT: And what happened since then?

MS. [][][][][][][][][]: Since then he hasn't contacted me. I haven't contacted him.

THE COURT: What made you change your mind for a restraining order then?

MS. [][][][][][][][][]: Because it's not right. It just wasn't right. When I went to the police department the first thing I said, I wasn't going to do a restraining order. But the first thing I went in there to tell the incident, I said, I just want it on record that this is what happened.

THE COURT: Were any charges filed?

MS. [][][][][][][][][]: At that time, the officer told me that, he took my report and he told me that because of the time that they can't —

THE COURT: When did you go to the police department?

MS. [][][][][][][][][]: I went to the police department the 28th, I believe, of February. And I just said can I just put it on record or does he have to get arrested or can he not just get arrested and we put it on record because he hasn't bothered me. And I was like I feel like I'm opening a can of worms. I don't want to aggravate the situation. I just want it on file that if he decided to get any rights

-¬THE COURT: All right. So what changed? All right so you did that the 28th.

59

MS. [][][][][][][][]: Yeah. Uh-huh.

THE COURT: What made you decide that you need the protection of a restraining order against him?

MS. [][][][][][][][]: Well, after the officer informed me, the officer said do you want to do a restraining order that day. And I said, well, . no, because he didn't, he hasn't contacted me.

THE COURT: Right.

And he said well you have the right to do that.

THE COURT: Right.

MS. [][][][][][][][]: Later on that night the officer called me and said because of the time, us or the police station, we can't press the charges, we can't sign the complaint. Only you would have to sign a complaint. 0o you want to do that. But I can't promise you he's not going to get arrested.

And I said is that the only way that I'm going to be able to put down what happened that day because I don't think that it's fair for him to just get off with it. He said, well if you want to do the complaint, but I would, it would be in your best right to go get a restraining order. Because if --

THE COURT: So he told you to get a restraining order?

MS. [][][][][][][][]: He asked, he said if I want to, he advised me. He said because if you do the complaint and he gets word of the complaint --

THE COURT: Bat why do you need a restraining order?

MS. [][][][][][][][]: Well I just was following what the officer had advised me to do. So I was taking the necessary steps in the order of what the officer had told me to do. And- then he said you do know he's going to get arrested. I said, you know what, okay.

THE COURT: All right. But that's not what I'm asking you.'- What made you go get a restraining order?

that if I'm going to sign a complaint, if I'm going to do a complaint, I should go do the restraining order at 10 Main Street. And I said, okay. And he said, if you feel like he's going to retaliate. And I said, you know what, I don't know what he would do if he figures out —

THE COURT: You just told me that you had never had any kind of incident like this before. this you don't expect to put their hands on you at all. And they do, do you find that person unpredictable. Yes. He's unpredictable. Because if

MS. [][][][][][][][]: Because the officer told me

MS. [][][][][][][][]: We never, no. Exactly. So if someone put —

THE COURT: And he hadn't contacted you since.

MS. [][][][][][][][]: - Exactly. But if someone goes after he put his hands on me and. I'm pregnant, and. because I didn't have an abortion he put his hands on me, what was I supposed to know two months, a month, three months down the line what he was going to do?

THE COURT: Okay. You said you have pictures.

MS. [][][][][][][][]: On my phone, yes.

THE COURT: Let me see. Show them first to the defendant/'

(Showing pictures to defendant and The Court.)

THE COURT: j-l. What are these pictures of?

MS. [][][][][][][]: My neck. When he put his hands on my neck. I took them the same day, that night. I should have took them the next day because my face and my neck, my neck was swollen. But that's the marks from us struggling in the house from my neck.

Because he only went at my neck. And I got like one ♦ * • ^ mark on my face.

THE COURT: Okay. Mr. Muhammad, you have the right to cross examine the plaintiff. That means you have the right to question her about her testimony.

I'll give you time to tell me what happened. But do you have any cross examination of her?

MR. MUHAMMAD: No.

THE COURT: Okay. Do you want to tell me what happened on January 5th?

MR. MUHAMMAD: I'm not even sure that January 5th is the date, which was the second time she came to see me. I've had an on again, off again physical relationship with for about two and a half years.

THE COURT: Physical   meaning sexual?

MR. MUHAMMAD: Exactly. In fact she's, I don't want to — the think is that the last time I saw her in the last, or even spoke to her in the last five months was the first week of December. When she contacted me I went to see her at her apartment. And I spent about six hours there. I left there at about —

SEVEN M.

THE COURT: You had a relationship with her?

MR. MUHAMMAD: Yeah.

THE COURT: Okay.

MR. MUHAMMAD: I left there at 1:30 in the morning because I don't spend the night when we do get together. I went home. She sent me a text message about eight days later saying that she needed to talk to me.

I said fine. Responded in a text, fine. Are you okay? She didn't answer right away. In the morning she sent another text saying, I'm late. So I said, okay. Come and see me.

THE COURT: You understood what I'm late meant?

MR. MUHAMMAD: Absolutely.-.

THE COURT: Okay. And what did you understand that tor. me an ?,>

MR. MUHAMMAD: That she thought that she might be pregnant.

THE COURT: Okay.

MR. MUHAMMAD: Now in the 18 or 19 or so times that we've been together, every time we took our clothes off I asked to count birth control pills. We discussed every time, without missing.

THE COURT: Well I think that Ms. made it clear that you didn't want to conceive a child.

MR. MUHAMMAD: Okay. No, no, that's not a problem. Okay. So, she came to see me the, I think it was the 2nd or 3rd day of January. She told me that she thought that she was pregnant. She brought an early pregnancy test. I made lunch.

She went in the bathroom. She came back. Showed me that the test said positive. I said okay. I kissed her on the forehead. We ate. We talked, watched television. I told her I have some place to be this afternoon. So I can't, you know, I can't be here with you all day. We agreed that we would stick to the original plan and why we would stick to it.

THE COURT: And what was the original plan?

MR. MUHAMMAD: The original plan that if either of our birth controls methods failed we would terminate pregnancy and continue our relationship and our friendship because I thought we were friends.

THE COURT: Do you have any other relationships at the same time as this?

MR. MUHAMMAD: No. Not a committed relationship. And I wasn't interested in having a committed relationship with her. And she was fine with that and that wasn't a problem.

So after we had that discussion she' 'said that she was going to contact, you know, the abortion clinic, She left without incident. I didn't speak to her the next day or the day after.

She contacted me and said she wanted to talk to me again. Again, I said fine, come over. She came over, sat down, and we started talking like we normally do. And I said, okay, so you know, I'll pay for everything, don't worry about anything. And, yes, I care about you and we will get through this together.

SEVEN M.

Same as anything else. She started talking about being deployed to Afghanistan. She started talking about all these other things and what she was afraid of. She was afraid of the procedure. She was afraid to go to Afghanistan.

And I looked at her and I was like look, I can't have anything to do with that. If you want to have the child, that's fine. You're on your own. I raised my daughter by myself from the time I was 19.

I divorced my wife and I'm raising my son by myself.

And I told her, I've been doing this since I was 19. I don't even have the capacity to be a parent again from the beginning. So if there's some financial responsibility, I will handle it. But I won't have anything to do with you and this anti-deployment. I won't have anything to do with you and the child when we discussed this almost 20 times.

She got upset. She screamed. She cried.

And just, you know, and I got upset. But I didn't get violent. I didn't get belligerent. There was none of that. I did walk her over to the sink. I did wash her face.

THE COURT: Why did she have the marks on her face?

MR. MUHAMMAD: I don't know anything about that. I don't know anything about that. There was no violence at all.

THE COURT: You didn't get scratched in the process too? Ms. [][][][][][][][][] said that you had, the two of you struggled.

MR. MUHAMMAD: I'm getting to that. When she was leaving, because if you remember the part of the story that she said was true,

I. did ask her to leave. I asked her to leave.

I walked over to the door and I opened the door.

Her two black, she had boots on. High heel black boots. They were sitting by the door because I don't allow shoes in my apartment. They were sitting by the door. The couch is near the door.

I picked up her coat, walked her coat outside to the rail, laid it on, told her to go. While I'm standing at the door I'm turned this way (indicating) because I didn't want to kiss her or anything. My arm is here (indicating) my hand is on the knob.

I reached, I grabbed her boots. I tried to hand her boots, she wouldn't take them. I dropped them. I turned my face. She hugged me and she grabbed me around the neck and she was crying. And I said listen, don't worry about anything. I forgive you.

You just let me know what you want to do. Whatever it is.I will take care of it.

When she was leaving she kept hugging me, she kept hugging me.

I told her leave. And I, you know, I didn't even push her. I just like, just leave, leave, leave, leave.

So finally she is grabbing me. She..«grabs me,

I didn't do anything. I'm six feet, I weight 225. I just heard her say something that was shocking to me and I saw it in the complaint. That there was a window broken. That I threw her through a window. That's what the complaint said.

SEVEN M.

I invite this Court to check my phone records. I invite the Court to talk to my landlord, to find out if any windows were broken or replaced in my apartment. Because every window in my apartment is intact 'and they're about 30 years old.

The bottom line is, the bottom line is I don't want to accuse her of trying to get off the deployment list. I don't know what's going on with her. But the bottom line is I told her I wouldn't have anything to do with her and the child would be a financial responsibility.

I have never ducked a responsibility in my life. I raised both of my children by myself. I invite the Court to check any of this out. Find out if she was on the deployment list and find out if the pregnancy took her off. Check the evidence.

And, no, I didn't have contact with her and I won't. And I never did. We don't go to dinner or nothing. We meet, we do what we do and that's it. I don't even spend the night.

When she came to me she was trying to create a relationship around this baby. I refused. And I continue to refuse. If there's some, if the child turns out to be mine, I will handle whatever responsibilities that are legally mine. But that's it. And she is the one who is unpredictable. I am very predictable.

And the other thing too, what you stated to me about how it would hinder my life from advancement,

I think that that's the motivation. I was arrested and I had to pay bail. So now I have to defend myself -¬THE COURT: You were arrested?

67

SURVIVING A FEMALE STALKER

MR. MUHAMMAD: I was arrested. The day after the police, the police came to my house at 12:30 at night while I was working on my new book.

They came and told me about this incident and the police officers that were there, I think it was Jason (phonetic) . He looked around the apartment. He looked to see if anything was broken.

He's shrugging his shoulders. He goes, look, you've got a problem. And if that baby turns out to be yours, you're going to have a further problem.

Next set of police officers came, 24 hours later,

12:30 and took me from my home. Domestic violence is something that police officers are very careful about because that's the time they get hurt. They don't get hurt when they arrest people for drugs. They don't get hurt, they get hurt on domestics.

So when they came, they came fired up. I had to calm them down. Me. And when they realized who I was and who I was in the community, they said, okay, listen, do what you've got to do. Get your stuff. I don't see any windows broken. I don't see any walls busted. None of that.

I fought for gloves. If I put someone

through a wall there's damage. If I throw someone through a window there's damage. If I pick someone up and slam them something gets broken. I would never do that.

THE COURT: Is there anything else you want to say?

MR. MUHAMMAD: No.

SEVEN M.

THE COURT: Ms. [][][][][][][], you may ask questions of the witness. Do you have any questions of him?

MS. [][][][][][][]: I'm kind of psyched.

THE COURT: What's so funny?

MS. [][][][][][][]: When did I inform you that I was on the deployment list?

MR. MUHAMMAD: Right after you told me that purposely getting a hot urine for marijuana didn't get 0 you off.

Of both parties and I've observed the demeanor of both witnesses. The defendant is animated. He's upset.

But he is clear in his testimony. And I have to weigh what makes more sense.

What concerns me is the plaintiff's demeanor, to be laughing during the entire time that she heard his testimony.

MS. [][][][][][][]: That purposely -- wow.

MR. MUHAMMAD: Your Honor, do I have to address her at all? I really —

THE COURT: You can answer through me. Do you have an other questions?

MR. MUHAMMAD: You're Honor, every single thing I've --

THE COURT: Wait, '-wait,- wait-t

THE COURT: Okay. I've heard the testimony

SURVIVING A FEMALE STALKER

There was an incident back in January, on or about January 5th, when the parties argued over the fact that the plaintiff was pregnant with what she believes is the defendant's baby. They had talked all through their two year relationship that the defendant refused to have a child.

When the plaintiff decided not to terminate the pregnancy she says she was assaulted by the defendant. She shows pictures marked as P-l of marks, bruises on her face and neck.

She says as she got up to leave the defendant grabbed her. He was hovering over her. But she admits that she was also upset, she was cursing at him, she was arguing. They were both arguing.

What concerns me is the plaintiff's testimony « • > » that she was slammed across a wall or on the ground and a window was broken. . .

I believe the defendant more than the * • «* plaintiff when he says that the police who came in and arrested him, even though the plaintiff testified that she did not file charges, nor did the police filed charges, nor was the defendant arrested. I did find out that that wasn't true.

I think that there was some sort of a scuffle here. *1 don't think that there was any intention on the part of the. defendant to assault the plaintiff.. He wanted, he told her to leave. She was grabbing at him. He might have pushed her away.

I don't find that there was an assault or a false imprisonment, or harassment. The plaintiff has not met her burden.

SEVEN M.

Even more importantly, this occurred in January 2011, January 5th. And the plaintiff didn't file for a restraining order until March 1st.

Silver v. Silver, that's at 387 Super at 112, it's an appellate division case, this Court must decide whether or not a predicate act of domestic violence was committed by the defendant. And I 1 don't find that.

But even so, the second prong of Silver is most important in this case. Whether a final restraining order is necessary to protect the plaintiff from immediate danger or further acts of domestic violence.

The Court should consider and make specific findings on the previous history. There is none. The plaintiff said she had never seen the defendant act this way. There was a mutual, I don't find that it was just the defendant who was angry. I believe it was the plaintiff who was angry as well, because she wanted him to help her out in this pregnancy.

And why, how, whether a restraining a final restraining order should protect the life, safety, or - well being of the plaintiff. After this incident the defendant wants nothing to do with the plaintiff. The plaintiff wants nothing to do with the defendant. He hasn't contacted her. There is no imminent danger here. The matter is dismissed.

Mr. Muhammad, you're going to probably get an application for child support. I heard Mr. Muhammad say he would be more than willing to support the child if it's his. The matter is dismissed. Please wait for my order.

MR. MUHAMMAD: Your Honor, may I ask one question?

THE COURT: Sure.

71

MR. MUHAMMAD: What about the criminal case?

with. I'm surprised there is a criminal case after hearing the testimony of the plaintiff that there was no criminal case. You'll have to speak with the police and go forward there.

THE CLERK: Have a seat in the back and wait for the order.

(Adjourned for the day.)

SEVEN M.

Certification

I the assigned transcriber, do hereby certify the foregoing transcript of proceedings on Court smart, from 9:06:51 to 9:38:08, is prepared in full compliance with the current Transcript Format for Judicial Proceedings and is a true and accurate non-compressed transcript of the proceedings as recorded.

009 (AAERT #00315)

(Date)

Conclusion

By Seven M.
the author

As human beings, we feel every possible emotion when we are in the throws of what we call real love. But, there is another story, this one. The one where only one of the two adults has a realistic picture of the future and there is no real love. Not that secure, nurturing, trust building kind of love. Not that kind. Not the kind where you don't have any secrets and you can hand each other the cell phone at any point in the day and not be worried when it rings. This is not that love. This is the bad kind. Not like the kind I just described. This is the bad kind because the bad behavior was displayed when there was any talk of ending the relationship. This is the bad story because not only is this behavior shown early, but while we're most off balance. When we are in a situation that we can't control.

While in this book we explored the male point of view, I will absolutely explore the female point of view in the next. I will always, always be fair. You need not worry about me Momma.

I am extremely heterosexual. Extremely. So, I will always be fair. Like I said earlier, most men don't have their shit together either. In fact, one of the subjects interviewed for this study turned to be the stalker himself. Told in his own words!

Everybody out here needs work. It's fucked up out here. For real. Now, I've got all kinds of words in my vocabulary and terms and phrases in my lexicon, but the fact is, we need real talk right now. I don't need to waste our time trying to impress you with that. We need to sit down somewhere and talk about it. Know what I mean? I don't mean a bunch of dudes sittin' around qualifying each other's bullshit, or a bunch of women sittin' around co-signing each other's emotional- estrogen based bullshit. I'm talking about brothers and sisters. We need to sit down and talk about it. Before we all have to wake up and face the fact that most of us don't have the tools to operate out here. We need to sit down and talk. That's what this work was about. To get people to sit down and talk. So that we could find ourselves in one of the subjects or characters in the book. Even if we didn't identify with any one character, it makes no matter, because we still identify with some of their behaviors. I know there were some brothers saying to themselves, "fuck subject so and so, that was his fault!" And at the same time be able to see themselves in some of his actions. You may be the type of dude where a woman could tell you from her own mouth that she's crazy and you still call her. Anything that happens to you after that, is your own damn fault and if you saw that in one of the characters, then you could identify and begin to fix your shit. Then, we could sit down and discuss with other people and begin to be better partners to each other. **Better partners to each other**.

I often hear people say, "it's gotta be fifty-fifty," but that fifty- fifty shit only works in the street when your doing business. Fifty-fifty doesn't work in a relationship. Nah, it's gotta be 100 and 100. I mean you were doing 100% before you met this person and now you want to cut your output/power to 50%, no. You put in one hundred percent and they put in one hundred percent and it's like getting a joint account, you don't lose shit.

Understand, you don't lose anything. This way, you still have all of your emotional capital in the bank. You're not emotionally bankrupt because you have consolidated your assets and now have more emotional currency and power. You both gave one hundred percent. When you go to a marriage counselor, one of the tests that they do and it's an excellent test, very revealing. They have your partner stand in front of you, eyes closed with their arms folded across their chest, then they ask your partner to fall back/free fall and they must trust that you will catch them. That you will not let them hit the ground. It's a trust exercise. I love that exercise because you can see the hesitation or the lack there of in the person who is supposed to fall back.

SEVEN M.

It tells you a lot about their relationship. This is the test that gives you the basics on how to start counseling. You start with trust. The majority of the problems we experience in relationships stem from trust. Not necessarily a lack there of, but trust. See, we have trust all fucked up.

We cheapen trust when we don't recognize or respect that trust only comes from repetition. From witnessing your partner in enough important situations that you can predict what they would do when you are not around to witness. Like I said, most of us have the concept of trust all fucked up. We don't know how to build trust. We know how to demand it; we know how to walk into a new situation and say, "I never did anything to you so, you should trust me." No! That shit never works. Theoretically it seems like the right shit but that doesn't work for humans and we need to face that as grownups. We need to face that. One of the most profound things I ever heard said about a relationship was in a movie about a slow talking boxer. His boxing trainer once said to him, "why do you love Adrienne so much? What's so great about Adrienne?" The boxer says, "I got gaps and she got gaps, and we fill each other's gaps."

That is the most profound thing I heard said about a relationship in a movie. See, some of that movie shit works in real life. A "perfect fit" is where there are no gaps. They filled each other's gaps. Now here's how we've got trust fucked up. You're supposed to build trust. You're not supposed to walk into a situation and demand it with no prior history of how this person behaves in different situations, with no experience with this person, what their preferences are, or what their love language is. You can't just walk in and demand trust because it takes time to build that. I truly believe that we wouldn't have the simple problems that we do if we took the time to build a solid foundation of trust. I've been in a couple situations where the second date was a trip to a doctor to be tested for HIV and STD's. This is the most powerful move you can make because you know immediately something personal and tangible about this person. During the test they reveal their real name and address and of course the most priceless info of all, what their sexual health rating is. Think about it in an ideal world, you should be able to make a grownup agreement with your mate so that you can first become "safe-sex partners." I know this sounds like it requires some type of commitment, and it does. It means that you commit to your "safe-sex partner" that he or she is the only person on the planet that you deal with sexually. It doesn't require that you go to parties, pay each other's bills or raise each other's children or pick each other up from work. It just means that when the human need for a certain level of intimate contact needs to be addressed, then you are my designated person. Being adult enough to make this first commitment is the first giant step toward building a trusting relationship. I wish that we could all take the time to build trust between men and women because we need each other so much. We really need each other.

Thank you for taking this journey with me.

Mr. Seven M

SEVEN M.

Thank you for buying my book and you can find my other books at Mrsevenm.com

#1 Amazon Author

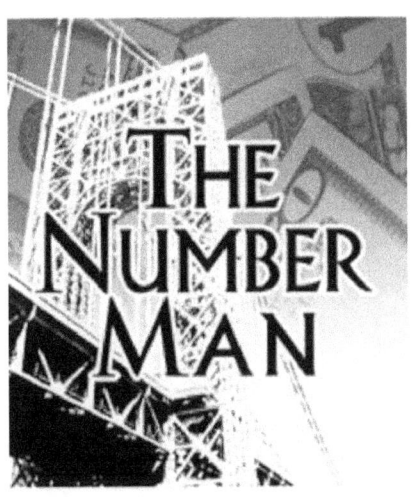

Mr. Seven M

Available now: Amazon.com, Barnes and Noble.com, Kindle E-Book, Google E-Books and Publish America and in bookstores everywhere!

Visit my website Mrsevenm.com to purchase 154th st. Audio Book 7 DAZE stage show

Follow me on Facebook @ Mr Seven M

www.ingramcontent.com/pod-product-compliance
Lightning Source LLC
Chambersburg PA
CBHW060133260626
47160CB00005B/2089